3: LUCE AND THE WEIRD KID

Mrs Bridge was just reading out the children's menu to all the quiet little guests when the door opened and my spirits sank, because there stood Eel, with a different lady this time.

At that moment three things happened. Mrs Bridge patted Ben's shoulder as if to say, "Don't worry, it's going to be all right;" the lady with Eel laid a hand on *his* shoulder as if to say, "Don't forget, best behaviour." And the third thing that happened was that Eel's wide, staring eyes locked into mine, and he stood stock still as if transfixed.

Also in the Café Club series by Ann Bryant

Have you read?
Go For It, Fen!
Leah Discovers Boys

Look out for:
Jaimini and the Web of Lies

The CAFÉ Club

3: LUCE AND THE WEIRD KID

Ann Bryant

Hippo

Thanks to Sue Hume for her invaluable help

Scholastic Children's Books,
Commonwealth House, 1–19 New Oxford Street,
London WC1A 1NU, UK
a division of Scholastic Ltd
London ~ New York ~ Toronto ~ Sydney ~ Auckland

First published by Scholastic Ltd, 1996

Copyright © Ann Bryant, 1996

ISBN 0 590 13426 4

Typeset by TW Typesetting, Midsomer Norton, Avon

Printed by Cox & Wyman Ltd, Reading, Berks.

All rights reserved

10 9 8 7 6 5 4 3 2 1

For John, Sue, Laura, Eleanor and Philippa

Chapter 1

Hi. I'm Lucy Edmunson, better known as Luce, the crazy one! If you could see me now you'd understand why I'm stuck with that label. My hair is a peculiar shade of purple and I'm not happy. My nose is a horrible shade of red – and runny. My brothers, Tim and Leo, the terrible twins, are getting seriously on my nerves and my friends are all at school unaware of my predicament.

If only I could contact my best friend Jaimini Riva, which you pronounce Jay-m-nee by the way. She's the brainy one. Unfortunately for me at the moment it's the academic sort of brain she's got, not the tele-pathic sort.

Jaimini, the lucky thing, is blessed not only with brains but with beauty. She's got coffee-cream skin that I would kill for. That's because her dad's black and her mum's white. Her hair is long, straight and black. Not like mine. I'm all freckles and curls. My hair wouldn't go straight if I paid it. I once tried ironing it, but I don't think I'll try that again in a hurry. I had to walk round with strange tufts of frizz on my head for ages. You'd think that would teach me a lesson, wouldn't you? But no chance, because here I am with purple hair. Anyway, I'll get back to that disaster in a minute. I'll just tell you about my other friends.

I'll start with Fen, because in a way she links us all. You see, her aunt Jan is the manageress of *The Café* in Cableden which is the town where we all live. To cut a long story short, Fen persuaded Jan to let the six of us friends work at the café on a rota basis. We work one day each, after school for a couple of hours, and every week a different one of us gets to do Saturday. That person works longer hours and earns more money. We're all thirteen-year-olds so we were lucky to get the job in the first place. It's great being part of the working world, but at times we have, shall we say, organizational problems. And right now is one of those times!

But I'm supposed to be telling you about Fen, aren't I? My mum, my teachers and my friends all say that I've got a butterfly mind and that I can't stick to one subject for more than thirty seconds at a time, so you'll have to forgive me if I keep bobbing off.

Anyway – Fen. Fenella Brooks is the ambitious one. She's slim and agile with brown hair to her shoulders, and bluey-grey eyes. She's very single-minded and determined, and can get quite stroppy at times if she believes strongly in something that's going wrong. Fen wears jeans and leggings a lot and looks really good in them.

Tash (Natasha Johnston) is Fen's best friend. She's the peacemaker. If I was like

Tash I'd never have to worry about anything because I wouldn't keep saying ridiculous things or making stupid moves. She's so sensible and kind and fair and sweet. It's impossible for anyone to dislike Tash. Her hair is dark, quite thick and short.

Leah Bryan is the musician. She's another member of the long straight hair brigade – lucky thing. Her hair is blonde and goes right down to her waist. She's always scraping it back into a bun or a pony-tail. She's got a very fragile, porcelain look, has Leah. Her face is lovely and calm. I'd love to look like her. That's my trouble. I'd love to look like so many people – almost anyone but me really!

Leah doesn't realize how good-looking she is. She's too wrapped up in her music. She's very, very talented. We're all convinced she's going to be famous one day. All except Leah herself, that is. She doesn't think she's very talented and gets fed up and wonders whether it's worth all the practising. She worries about everything, which is crazy, because unlike me, she hardly ever gets into scrapes.

4

Her best friend is Andy. Andy is amazing. Andy is the daring one. And I mean *daring*! There's nothing she wouldn't dare to do. The funny thing is she's the smallest of us all and is really petite with lovely bone structure, big brown eyes and *very* short dark hair.

Andy's mum is French and her dad is English, but funnily enough he works in France and would really like to live there. That's where he met Andy's mum in the first place, you see. Andy's real name is Agnès. It's a French name so you pronounce it Ann-yes, which sounds much nicer than the English pronunciation, doesn't it? We all say Andy because it's easier and it suits her better. She ought to be a spy when she grows up. She can move so quickly and silently, and she's excellent at PE.

Come to think of it, she's probably doing netball right now. Perhaps I should sneak out of the house and up to school and try to attract her attention. The road's not *that* far away from the netball courts. No, I can't do that because one – my purple hair might just possibly draw attention to me and two – my brothers (the aforementioned wonder twins Leo and Tim aged eight) have made any escape on my part such an expensive prospect that it's right out of the question.

Let me start at the beginning. I am stuck at home with a stinker of a cold. And so are they. We are all housebound. I'm actually supposed to be bed-ridden, but I'm out of bed, sitting on my bedroom floor and wondering what to do. You see, it's my turn at the café today, and because I wasn't at school yesterday and Mum said I definitely wouldn't be well enough to cope with school today, Fen phoned me up and offered to do my café duty for me, but I, like a fool said, "Don't worry, I'm doing the work even if I'm *not* at school. We hardly ever see any of the teachers at the café so the chances of my getting caught are minute. Even if there *did* happen to be a teacher in there, they'd probably never realize I hadn't been at school that day."

That was all very well but I hadn't reckoned with Mum. It was just before lunch when we had this conversation…

"I'm fine, Mum, honestly. I'm feeling so much better now. I'll definitely go to school tomorrow, so it'll be no problem working at the café at four o'clock today."

"If you're not well enough to go to school, Lucy, you're not well enough to work, and that is that."

"But it's only for a couple of hours."

"A couple of hours is hard work when you should be gaining your strength for tomorrow."

"But that's what I'll be doing. I'll be building it up for tomorrow…"

"Look, Lucy, you cannot work in a place which serves food when your nose is continually running. You'll have to get one of the others to do your duty."

"I can't. It's too late now."

"Well, then you'll just have to phone Jan and apologize, and as soon as the others get home phone round until you find one of them who can at least cover for the second part of your duty."

"Oh, Mum…" I said in a desperate hopeless whine.

"It's your own fault," was Mum's parting shot. That made me really mad because I reckon it was *her* fault for being so inflexible. It was at that moment that I decided there was nothing for it. I would have to go to work without Mum knowing I'd even left the house.

Had my two brothers not been at home I think I would have risked telling Mum I was going to bed for a bit, and told her not to disturb me. She is usually so busy that she forgets about me when I'm not actually in the same room as her. She's either in the kitchen getting weird and wonderful dishes together – my mum's a caterer, you see – or otherwise out in the garden which she loves, or writing poetry which she also loves, or doing one of the other millions of things she does in life.

So escaping for a couple of hours shouldn't have been a problem. Except, of course, that my brothers – bless their cotton socks – were bound to give the game away. Like this…

"Mum, what time's Luce coming back?"

"What do you mean, coming back? She hasn't gone anywhere, has she?"

"Whoops…"

So I decided to have a word with the little darlings.

"Listen, you two, don't you dare breathe a word to Mum about the fact that I've gone out, or I'll personally land you in so much trouble that you'll be grounded with no pocket money for a whole month."

"Why? Where are you going?" Tim wanted to know.

"None of your business."

"It's the café, isn't it?" said Leo, Mr Wisdom.

"OK, it's the café. Now promise me you'll keep shtum."

"It'd be much easier to keep shtum if you made it worth our while." This was from Tim, Mr Greedy.

"Twenty pence each. No more."

"Twenty pence! You've got to be kidding! Seventy-five pence at least," announced Leo.

"Each," added Tim. (Like I said, Mr Greedy.)

"Oh, go on, then," I said, reluctantly handing over the one pound fifty that I'd got all ready because I knew they'd never do it for any less. "It's hardly worth going to work now," I added grumpily.

"You'd only get found out if we weren't here. At least this way we can help to distract Mum's attention."

"Yes, like if we see her about to go into your room with a pile of ironing, we can offer to take the pile in for her."

"Hmm," I said doubtfully, as a picture of Tim generously helping Mum with her ironing pile, came into my head. "Just don't overdo it, will you?" I cautioned them. "Otherwise she'd instantly be suspicious."

"We won't, never fear," they grinned. "You'll need some sort of disguise, you know," Leo commented. "If anybody tells Mum that they saw you, it'll be curtains for you."

I hadn't thought about Mum getting to hear, only about the teachers. So that's when

I decided to dye my hair, to disguise myself. We'd got two or three hair colourants in the house because Mum did her own hair regularly at home. It was a blonde colour and I was certain it was supposed to rinse out so it would be perfect. Jan would accept the new colour as me experimenting. I was always experimenting with clothes, so hair wasn't much different.

There were only two packets left in the bathroom cabinet so I had to be sure to get it right first time, otherwise Mum would wonder how come she was right out of hair colourants and didn't even remember using up the last one. I scanned the instructions very quickly because I was impatient to get my new colour, and I didn't see the word "half" written just in front of "an hour". So, as I've told you, my hair came out a revolting purple colour. I stood under the shower frantically trying to wash the awful colour out but each time I looked in the mirror, there was absolutely no change in my ghastly appearance.

"Put a scarf on," giggled Tim.

"Or put a stocking over your head," spluttered Leo.

"Put a sock in it, both of you," I hit back at them. "Whose barmy idea was it anyway, that I should disguise myself?" I demanded angrily.

In the end I wrapped a long Indian scarf round my head so none of my hair showed, and hoped that Jan wouldn't object to it. She'd once told me off about wearing big loopy earrings, so she might think it wasn't subdued enough for the "girl-working-in-the-café" image. Well, there was nothing for it. The damage was done.

"Now, don't forget," I hissed at the terrible twins as I was about to leave the house. "I have paid you good money to do a good job, and when I get back I do *not* want to find that Mum has any idea that I haven't been safely installed in my bedroom all afternoon. *Capiche?*"

They nodded obediently and I slipped out of the front door and zipped off down the road.

"Hey, it's Gipsy Rose Lee," Kevin the chef announced as I opened the back door into the kitchen at four o'clock precisely. "No, I tell a lie, it's a very attractive young lady auditioning for the part of Rudolph the Red-Nosed Reindeer!" He then guffawed loudly at his own wit while sifting fine breadcrumbs of scone mixture through his fingers.

"Ha, ha, 'scuse me while I die of laughter," I retorted crossly.

"Only joking," he grinned. "It's very er … nice," he added unconvincingly. "Have you dyed your hair purple or something?"

I blushed furiously because he'd unwittingly hit the nail right on the head.

"You have, haven't you?" he persisted, beginning to crack up. "I'm right, aren't I?" With that he quickly rinsed his fingers under the tap, wiped them briefly on his apron, and tweaked at the edge of my scarf to try to see what lay underneath.

"Get off," I squealed, clutching my scarf tight to my head, and that's when Jan walked in.

"Why is it that trouble seeks you out and dogs your footsteps, young lady?" she asked in exasperation. "What's the matter now? You can take that scarf off for a start."

"I c-can't. That's the … problem," I stammered, "but I do look neat, don't I? Look – polished shoes – no earrings."

"Red nose," Kevin dropped in just loudly enough for me to hear. Then Mark came in. It's always Mark or Becky on duty at the same time as one of us girls. Mark's only about seventeen, and really nice.

"Nineteen ninety-six," he said in a very posh voice, "latest fashion – turbans are *in*, ladies."

"Be quiet, Mark," Jan snapped. "This isn't a laughing matter. Why can't you take the scarf off?" she demanded of me.

I decided the truth was in order before she got really mad.

"Because my hair's purple," I said flatly.

There was a short pause, then Mark and Kevin fell about laughing and Jan went extremely tight-lipped. I looked her square in the face and didn't say a word, just waited for the inevitable telling off. You can imagine my surprise when her tight lips transformed into a wide grin and she laughed as hard as Kevin and Mark.

"Oh, Lucy," she finally spluttered, "you really are the limit. I won't ask you how you managed this latest incredible feat. I'll turn a blind eye this once – just this once, mind. Now, washing-up! Get to it!" And I did. Only I had to keep breaking off to dry my hands and blow my nose.

"You should be at home in bed, young lady," Jan commented with a frown a little later when I did a particularly big blow and then sighed without thinking.

"No, I'm OK, honestly."

"Well, there are a few drinks orders mounting up in there. Are you up to seeing to them? Just line them up on the trays in the right order."

"Oh, yes, no problem," I assured her, and I swung confidently through the door to the café, forgetting all about my rather strange appearance.

In fact the first I thought about it was when I heard a snigger from the corner table. "Huh, I won't even bother to look," I said to myself, lifting my chin to show I didn't care. "Just because someone is sniggering it doesn't mean that they're sniggering at me, after all."

But then I heard the words "Egyptian mummy" and I knew that someone was definitely finding my scarf mega amusing. I glanced up as nonchalantly as I could and noticed a boy of about eight, I guess, sitting with a woman who was probably his mother. There were a couple of women who had obviously been shopping sitting at the next table, so the big wit who'd commented on my scarf must have been the boy. At that moment he glanced up and hesitated, then gave me a smile. I didn't alter my expression one iota. I just continued milkshaking and cappuccinoing as though nothing had happened.

"Well done," whispered Mark out of the side of his mouth, as he glided past the counter where I was working.

"Definitely getting very mature," Jan agreed later in the kitchen when Mark had explained about the eight-year-old comic.

"Evil little toad," I said.

"Don't be too hard on him, Lucy, he may have just been giving you a perfectly friendly smile."

"Who's been giving you perfectly friendly smiles, Luce?"

We all turned round to see who had spoken, and there stood Jaimini. I ran over and gave her a hug.

"Hi, Luce, are you OK?"

"Yes, fine," I said, changing my expression to a strong warning look, because I didn't want Jan to know I hadn't been at school. "Oh, you mean this?" I added, touching my scarf and rolling my eyes.

"You haven't dyed it, have you?" she asked.

"Yes," Kevin answered before I could say a word. "This month's hair colour, a delightful shade of purple."

I whacked him in the ribs for saying that, while Jaimini gasped.

Kevin is in his early twenties. He's very fit and *very* attractive and not married. I suppose Jaimini is right. She's always telling me he's far too old for me, but sometimes when he's working away I just can't take my eyes off him.

As soon as Jaimini and I were on our own, apart from Kevin, who couldn't possibly have heard us with all the clatter he was making, I showed Jaimini my hair, and then found out why she'd turned up at the café.

"I called in at your place before I came here. The boys are doing an excellent job, Luce. Tim met me at the door before I'd even knocked, because he'd been keeping a look out just in case I turned up. He ushered me into your room talking loudly about how you might be asleep, and giving me slow motion broad winks. I decided to let him ramble on because I couldn't work out what was happening.

"When we got inside your room, he shut the door firmly and clapped a hand over my mouth. It was a good job he did, because I was just about to demand loudly where you were, and your mum was coming up the stairs. Anyway, he then gave me a lot of information in a few gunshot sentences… 'She's at the café. She sneaked out. Mum doesn't know. We're keeping guard. Look.' And he shoved seventy-five pence under my nose, looking as proud as if you'd given him seventy-five pounds!

"At that moment the phone rang. It only just rang for the teeniest micro-second before it stopped. In fact I wasn't even sure that I'd not been hearing things. In no time at all, there was a strange knocking at the door – two slow and three quick taps, then Tim opened the door the tiniest crack and in slithered Leo!

"'That was Fen on the phone for Luce,' Leo told Tim as though I wasn't there at all. I really think they fancy themselves as special agents, you know, Luce… I asked them what Fen wanted and apparently she just wanted to check you were at the café, and Leo had assured her you were."

I couldn't help giggling at Jaimini's description of Tim and Leo carrying out the task I'd set them. It was really clever of them to have thought about answering the phone before Mum could get to it, and about keeping a look out for visitors to the house.

"The bad news," Jaimini said, looking rather grave, "is that your charming brothers have had enough of their job and they instructed me to tell you that if you didn't get back by ten past five, they'd demand overtime pay, and if you refused to pay it, they'd tell your mum that you'd sneaked out."

"The nasty little toe-rags," I commented fiercely.

"But the good news is that your best friend is here to step into the breach, so you can go now and I'll finish off your duty."

"Oh, Jaimes, you're such a gem," I told her while giving her another hug.

"Go on, you'd better run. It's nearly five o'clock."

"Oh, no, my hair!" I wailed. "I was going to go to the chemist and buy some more really strong dye to get my hair back to its proper colour. Surely the boys won't mind if I'm ten minutes late."

"I think they *will* actually, Luce, because there's a programme that starts at ten past five. That's why they want you back by then, so they can watch it in peace, without having to stand by the phone and keep an eye on your mum's whereabouts the whole time."

"Oh," I moaned. "What about my hair?"

"Why did you dye it in the first place?"

"Because I wanted a disguise in case any teachers saw me in here and started asking questions about why I wasn't at school. I wish I hadn't bothered now."

"That scarf is a big enough disguise. You look completely different without any hair showing."

"I think I'd better skip the chemist. If I keep washing my hair tonight it might be OK by tomorrow, and anyway I can't afford to pay them any more money."

I rushed off quickly leaving Jaimini to explain my sudden disappearance to Jan. It was easy running the first hundred metres, but not long after that I began to feel hot and tired, and I don't usually get puffed out that soon. It's because I'm not well, I thought to myself, slowing down and taking deep breaths. It was then that I could have sworn I heard someone walking behind me. I turned round but there was not a soul in sight.

Must have imagined it, I told myself lightly. All the same I kept my ears open and tried not to tread too noisily. After a few seconds I got the same feeling again. There was definitely someone behind me. I turned round very quickly this time and sure enough there was a boy. He looked about eight or nine, but I couldn't tell much more about him because he immediately bent down to tie up his shoe-lace. I was beginning to feel rather curious by now – not afraid or anything, after all it was only a boy, but I couldn't work out why he didn't want me to see him.

When I got to my house the front door opened a fraction and Leo's face appeared.

"Psst!" he hissed. "Come in quick! Mum's in the sitting room."

Just before the door closed behind me I looked back into the street and saw the boy.

He turned round as soon as he realized I was looking but he wasn't quick enough. I caught a glimpse of his face. It was the same boy who had taken the mickey out of my scarf at the café, and then had the cheek to smile at me.

Leo whispered hurriedly that he didn't think Mum suspected anything although she had tried to go into my room twice but the boys had managed to sidetrack her and she'd never actually gone in.

"Thanks Leo," I whispered, "you've both done a good job. I'll remember you in my will. But right now I'd better get into my room, quick."

But before I could, the living room door opened and Mum came out.

Chapter 2

"I thought you were asleep in bed."

"Hi, Mum," I said, through a big fake yawn as I stretched my arms slowly above my head. It's easy to fake a yawn because half-way through the fake it turns into a real one if you concentrate hard enough – you ought to try it.

"Was that the front door I heard?"

"Yes," Leo popped straight back at her. "I saw this boy from our class through the window upstairs, so I was just calling out 'Hi' to him."

I glanced at Leo. That was very glib, I thought. And then it occurred to me that perhaps he really was from Leo's class at school. But if that was the case why did the boy go to such lengths to keep himself hidden from me?

Mum looked at her watch at that point and her face took on a puzzled frown. I knew exactly how her mind was working. She didn't believe Leo. She thought it was me getting up to something sneaky, coming back in through the front door, but she couldn't work out why I was back from the café at only ten past five, as I wouldn't have left half-way through my duty.

"You're looking very guilty, Lucy," she said, fixing a beady eye on me and touching my cheek with the back of her hand. It obviously felt cold. "I wasn't born yesterday, you know. Where have you been?" This time she looked cross.

"Um…" I was about to confess when I had a sudden burst of inspiration.

"I nipped out to the corner shop to see if they'd got any sort of hair products…"

Her frown was deepening. She transferred

her weight to the other leg, her arms folded, her head tilted. This was her "You-don't-expect-me-to-believe-*that*!" pose. But I was feeling confident now and I was about to go for the clincher. Very slowly and dramatically I pulled the scarf off my head, and she shot so far into the air, I thought she'd found a new way of getting upstairs. Both her hands flew to her mouth and she did a little scream.

"Your hair! It's purple! I mean it's ... it's *purple*!" she repeated with as much horror as if I'd had snakes writhing from my scalp like Medusa.

"I was bored, you see, and I was just looking in the mirror and thinking how awful my hair looked, when I suddenly thought I'd try to make it more blondey-golden, but I must have done something wrong... Sorry, Mum!"

My remorse obviously came over well, or maybe she was just relieved to have the truth about my little excursion – little did she know – but she started acting like I would imagine a Mrs Dormouse character to act. She bustled me upstairs with all sorts of sighing and tutting noises, slung a towel round my shoulders, and before the wash basin was even full she shoved my head down and began vigorously tipping water from the toothbrush mug over my hair. This was followed by a hard massaging of my scalp with our strongest shampoo.

I couldn't help noticing that after a bit the sighs and tuts turned to gasps of horror and "Omigods". "What?" I asked, beginning to feel my knees trembling.

"It's falling out!" she shrieked. "Great handfuls of it. Look!"

I tried to turn my head sideways to look but she clamped me back down again.

"So it is," said Tim, who I hadn't realized was also present for the spectacle.

"Let me see, Mum," I said, beginning to feel worried. She squeezed what remained of my hair and wrapped it in a towel as my stiff neck straightened up. Then she did the gentlest rubbing she could, as though any-thing more vigorous might cause the last clinging hairs to lose their roots and slide helplessly into the basin. As the towel came down my shoulders I was petrified as to what it would reveal.

Wide-eyed I stared into the bathroom mirror, aware that Tim, Leo and Mum were also staring. Then Mum and I let out long sighs of relief. The damage was nowhere near as bad as we'd feared. I've already explained that my hair is very thick, curly and wiry. Well, obviously with hair like that, you can afford to lose quite a lot before any visible damage is done. Apart from the awful colour which hadn't changed at all, my hair actually looked better than usual.

"Stop grinning at yourself," said Leo.

"Yeah, there's a name for people like you. It's er … daffodil."

Mum and I smiled because he'd got the wrong flower.

"No, it's not, it's narcotics," Leo told his brother in an authoritative tone.

"I think you mean Narcissus," Mum corrected them both, trying not to laugh.

That meant that I was very vain, but I

couldn't be bothered to protest about this insult, and anyway they'd lost interest by then and Tim had disappeared into his room.

"What's *he* doing here?" came his strident tones a few seconds later.

"I'm nipping out to the chemist," Mum said. "It's late night closing tonight."

"Thanks, Mum," I said quickly, because I was actually more interested in what Tim had just said. Leo had joined his brother in his room.

"Huh! Eel. I saw him when Luce got back from the c…"

I held my breath.

"…corner shop."

I let out my breath.

"What's he doing here?"

"He'd better not be up to anything."

I went into Tim's room and looked out of the window without getting too close. Mum was going out of the front door.

"Who is he?" I whispered to Tim.

"A new kid at our school. Nobody likes him. He's called Eel Perry."

"That's a peculiar name."

"He's not really called Eel, but he's always in scrapes – I mean *big* scrapes," Leo explained, "but somehow he always slips out of trouble. The teachers must be blind or something."

"We call him Eel because he's as slippery as an eel, you see," Tim went on. The twins always took turns when it came to explanations. Much as they got on my nerves at times, I couldn't help feeling a rush of affection for them as they stood there on their thin little legs with their identical faces looking anxiously out at Eel, who was kicking stones and walking up and down.

"Get back! He's looking up here," Tim said in an urgent voice.

"What's the big deal? Why don't you call out to him? Is he in your class?"

"Well, not exactly. He's in the parallel class," Leo said.

"Thank goodness," they both added together.

"We don't like him," Tim went on, stating the obvious.

"Nobody does," Leo added, and they went scooting downstairs without saying anything more. They often did that – acted absolutely at the same moment without a single word being spoken. It was almost as though they shared a brain between them, which made all the joint decisions, so it wasn't necessary to tell the other one what they'd decided to do.

They're not actually my real brothers, Tim and Leo. They're my half-brothers. They belong to Mum and my stepdad, and we all live together. My proper dad lives quite a way away. He moved when he and Mum got divorced. I see him every few weekends. He and his new wife, Sally, have got a son called Edward and a daughter called Colette.

My stepfather, who's really nice, is called Terry and he's got two sons from his first marriage. They're called James and Jon. James is nineteen and Jon is twenty-one. Neither of them lives with us but they often come and visit or stay for a short while. Our house is quite big, quite old, needs painting and isn't very tidy, mainly because of the twins. When James and Jon come to stay, Leo moves into Tim's room. We're quite a muddly sort of family but I like it like that.

When Jaimini comes here she thinks she's entered another century or another planet or something because it's all so different from what she's used to. She's an only child, and her house is small and pristine clean and tidy. When I go there I get some lovely peace and quiet. It's all so calm and relaxing.

Even *my* house seemed fairly calm and relaxing at this moment, because I was alone upstairs. Well – almost alone. That boy Eel seemed to be practically in the house with me, his presence was so strong. I rubbed my hair gently and stared at him for the next two or three minutes, wondering what on earth he was doing outside our house, apart from kicking stones. Eventually he looked at his watch, gave one more glance up at the window, which made me duck out of sight, then walked away. He had a PE bag or something with him and he kept clouting the wall with it as he walked along. There was something very odd about young Eel, and I wasn't at all surprised that he was not a popular boy.

The next day I woke up feeling much better. A glance in the mirror put me on top of the world. The previous evening Mum had come back from the chemist with the hair colourant, and my hair was now the most wonderful colour. It was just a fraction blonder than it usually is. The colourant had taken the purple look away – *and* the auburn look, come to think of it! Also my nose had returned to its normal colour and stopped running.

"Oh, Luce, you look so sophisticated," Jaimini said, as we sat round at the bottom of the netball courts, our favourite outdoor meeting spot.

"You look like a film star," Leah added, which was a massive compliment because if anyone round here looks like a film star, it's Leah!

"You look lovely," Tash agreed with a smile, "but then I thought you looked lovely with your natural colour, too."

Fen agreed with Tash. "Your natural colour is *you*, Luce. It's all part of your crazy character. This colour is brilliant, of course, but now you're just one of the crowd."

"I agree with Fen," Andy said.

"Well, either way, I can tell you it's a ton better than purple!"

We all laughed, then Jaimini started to tell us what had happened the previous day at the café. The others already knew that Jaimini had taken over from me half-way through.

"It was amazing, Luce. I went into the café about five minutes after you'd gone, and the very first thing I was aware of was this boy…"

"Eel…" I whispered, talking to myself really.

"Do you know him?"

"No … go on…"

"His eyes followed me everywhere, and his mum kept telling him to turn round and stop staring and things, but he either ignored her or knocked her hand away if she dared to touch him. I could tell she was trying to keep calm and didn't want a scene, and I could also tell that this kid was like a dormant volcano. His mum was probably dreading the volcano erupting. Eventually she smiled at me and called me over.

" 'Could I have another cup of tea and also an iced bun, please?' she asked me. She sounded so nice and sensible. I couldn't work out how she could have brought up her son to be so badly behaved, because by then he'd deliberately kicked the table which made the milk jug tip over, and that made a right mess, I can tell you.

"Anyway, I smiled at the woman and thought I'd get on with the order before the boy made any racist comments…"

"Actually he called me an Egyptian mummy – that's pretty racist, isn't it?" I said.

The others laughed but Jaimini was looking thoughtful.

"Are you sure he did?"

"Pretty sure. Why?"

"Because there were two women at the table next to him and they were poring over a fashion magazine, and I actually heard one of them say, 'It's revolting, but not as bad as that girl on page twenty-six with the body scarf who looked like an Egyptian mummy.' Then they both went into hysterics."

"So it was those women looking at a magazine…" I said, thoughtfully. "Nothing to do with me … and nothing to do with Eel."

"Carry on with what happened," Fen urged Jaimini, ever impatient.

"Well, thank goodness, he didn't say anything racist, but he obviously wasn't happy about something, because he grabbed my apron and said, 'Where's that other girl?' His mother then calmly told him to say, 'Excuse me, please,' but the boy ignored her and carried on talking to me in the most accusing tones as though I'd bumped you off and taken your place or something. 'She's gone, hasn't she?' he demanded.

"'Yes she has,' I told him. 'I've taken over from her. Do you know her?'

"He didn't answer, just leapt up from the table as though he was the police and he'd just received a tip-off about an escaped criminal.

His mother gave me an apologetic, but still very calm and controlled, smile, quickly laid the exact money on the table and walked briskly out after him. It was weird. It was almost as though she had the money ready – you know – just in case the kid did a runner."

"So did he catch up with you, Luce?" asked Andy.

"Yes, he did. He must have shaken his mother off. What a cunning little kid. No wonder they call him Eel."

"Who calls him Eel? Do you know him?" the others wanted to know.

So I quickly finished off Jaimini's story and we were all left wondering why on earth an eight-year-old boy I didn't know from Adam would want to follow me.

"If he knows your brothers, maybe he also knows that you're their sister, and he thought if he followed you he could find out where they lived," Fen suggested.

"Yeah. Maybe he's got something against them," Andy suggested.

"I'm sure nobody could have anything

against Tim and Leo," said Tash, kindly as always. "They're such sweet boys."

"Get real, Tash. They're revolting little nerds," I said and the others laughed – even Tash.

"Anyway, I think I ought to warn you, Leah, that tomorrow, Saturday, there's going to be a party for twelve of the lovely eight-year-old species, and it's *you* on duty!" Jaimini announced.

"Oh, no! Oh, spare me!" wailed Leah. "I can't handle twelve eight-year-old kids."

"'Fraid you'll have to. The mother – a Mrs Bridge – phoned and reserved a table for birthday boy Ben and his eleven friends. Six boys, six girls."

"Oh, Andy," begged Leah, "you don't want to swap duties, do you?"

"I daren't. My dad's almost definitely coming back this evening, so I'd better make sure I'm nowhere near the café this weekend."

Andy's dad doesn't actually realize she works at the café yet because Andy and her mum are waiting for the right moment to tell him. He's very strict and quite frightening, and when Andy's mum mentioned the café idea to him in the first place, he put his foot down and said, "Absolutely not!"

I've already told you that Andy's dad works in France, well, he'd really like to live in France, but her mother fell in love with England the very first time she came over here on a trip, so she doesn't want to go back to France. Andy always says her dad's bark is worse than his bite, but the rest of us are all terrified of him, though we'd never tell Andy that. I once said that nothing scares Andy. Well, I was wrong. One thing scares her – her dad.

"Oh, Tash, dearest Tash," continued Leah on bended knee with praying hands, "please say you'll do Saturday duty for me…"

"Oh, Leah, I would if I possibly could but we're going away to see some friends of the family all day Saturday."

"Who's working today?" Leah asked in a rush.

"Luce and I are sharing again, because it's really me but I did half of yesterday," said

Jaimini.

"I'll tell you what, I'll do today and you two share tomorrow? How about that?" Leah proposed enthusiastically.

Jaimini and I looked at each other, then Jaimini pulled a face. "I feel the same as you do about trying to keep a load of eight-year-olds under control. I mean, what do you do if they start flicking jelly or something?"

"You take the jelly away from them and tell them that if they carry on like that, you'll take the whole lot away from them – even if it *has* been paid for."

Everybody stopped and stared when I said that.

"Luce, you are a natural," breathed Leah. "Of course, you know exactly how to handle eight-year-olds with brothers like yours."

"OK. OK. Flattery'll get you anywhere you want. I'll do the whole Saturday duty and you two can share today."

"You're an angel," Leah told me, giving me an impulsive hug.

* * *

So that's how I came to be in the café surrounded by balloons and streamers, heaping party poppers and funny hats on to bright Solar Samson napkins – the latest craze for the boys – and pastel coloured Tressida napkins – the latest craze for the girls. I knew all about Solar Samson from Leo and Tim, and Fen had filled me in on Tressida, super businesswoman with loads of power outfits and smart briefcases, that all the girls loved to collect.

"How are you getting on, pet?" Jan asked me, rushing in and setting tumblers at every place.

"Just about done it," I told her as I added another couple of chairs to make twelve.

"They'll be here any minute," Jan added, looking at her watch. "And I only hope that they're not so noisy that they put other customers off."

"Do you want me to take away the party poppers?" I asked her with a grin.

"No, just encourage them to let them all off at the beginning, then that'll be the end of that. Uh-oh! Here comes birthday boy."

I looked up and there stood a very neat and respectable boy in beautifully pressed jeans, a crisp white shirt and a little waistcoat. His hair was shiny and tidy, and his whole appearance made me wonder how such a nice-looking boy could possibly be friendly with my two ruffian brothers who were also invited to the birthday tea.

Just as I was thinking that, Leo and Tim appeared. Mum more or less shoved them through the door, giving them last minute whispered instructions to say thank you and be polite. The twins weren't taking any notice of her. They were nodding dutifully, but all the while their eyes were on the bright, promising-looking table. She waved at me and disappeared.

"Right, action stations," Jan announced as six more children came pouring in through the door.

"Ben's parents *are* staying, aren't they?" I checked anxiously with Jan.

"Oh yes, don't worry. They seem very nice. They're called Mr and Mrs Bridge."

There were three more children still to come. Leo was walking round the table, picking up every single party popper, examining it and replacing it. Goodness only knows what he was hoping to find. Tim was head to head with another boy, admiring whatever was in the other boy's upturned palm. Both boys looked at each other gravely, then looked back at the contents of the hand. I thought I'd better get wise and check this one out. I approached from behind and peered over their heads. It was a trick spider – a very realistic one. The only reason I didn't scream was because I was expecting something even worse.

"Two more," said Becky, who works in the café whenever Mark doesn't. She ushered two little girls over to the table, with a rather fixed grin on her face. My brothers are already eight, but birthday boy, Ben Bridge, was celebrating his eighth birthday and quite a few of the guests were only seven.

"Right, I think we can all sit down now," Ben's mother announced, clapping her hands and smiling round. I was getting ready to intervene if there was any fighting about where to sit, but I needn't have worried because these children were so well behaved, sensible and quiet. Tim and Leo were probably the most mischievous children there, and I knew very well how to cope with them. But for some reason or other, young Ben, who was covered with "I'M 8" badges, was looking very anxious and ill at ease. His mother had been twittering around him for ages and even his father seemed quite fussy.

"Let's just wait for Hal before we put the hats on, shall we?" Mrs Bridge said with another smile round the table. Eleven pairs of eyes looked solemnly back at her.

"Shall I give you and Mr Bridge a menu?" I asked her. "Then you can be choosing."

"Oh, yes please, good idea," she responded enthusiastically. The children seemed to sit up a little with the thought of food, but I couldn't say they were the most cheerful bunch of little souls I'd ever come across. I got out my second writing pad, which I had brought specially for this occasion, because I knew from experience how often children change their minds, so I thought I'd do a rough copy of the orders first and set it out in the order that they were seated round the table, so that I wouldn't have any problem remembering who had ordered what. Jan had been really impressed when I'd told her my cunning little plan. "There's hope for you yet," she had teased me.

Mrs Bridge was just reading out the children's menu to all the quiet little guests when the door opened and my spirits sank, because there stood Eel, with a different lady this time.

At that moment three things happened. Mrs Bridge patted Ben's shoulder as if to say, "Don't worry, it's going to be all right;" the lady with Eel laid a hand on *his* shoulder as if to say, "Don't forget, best behaviour." And the third thing that happened was that Eel's wide, staring eyes locked into mine, and he stood stock still as if transfixed.

Chapter 3

I turned my attention to a little girl with blonde curls who had been tapping my hand without my realizing it.

"Will we be getting tomato ketchup, Miss?"

"Yes, of course you will, and don't call me Miss," I told her as gently as I could.

"What shall I call you then?"

I suddenly felt very irritated by this perfectly innocent child. "You can call me Father Christmas if you want. Anything but Miss, OK?"

She giggled as I turned to go and get the tomato ketchup.

"Can I have some brown sauce please,

Father Christmas?" piped up the boy sitting next to blondey. I presumed that he didn't have any pressing need for the brown sauce as he then turned to his neighbours on either side and guffawed heartily at his own wit. As it happened both neighbours had their attention on other things, so the boy in the middle finished up looking rather silly.

I was still grinning to myself about this as I came back with the tomato ketchup. My eyes happened to rest on Eel. His transfixed gaze had not altered. Our eyes met. What was it with this kid? I decided to confront him. His mother, or whoever she was, was still here and looked as though she was going to stay throughout the meal, thank goodness, but at that moment she was engrossed in helping Mrs Bridge sort the orders out.

"Hello," I said to Eel in a friendly voice as I bent down beside him.

"Where's your scarf? You look different without your scarf," he told me almost fiercely. This was hardly the type of opener I expected from a boy of his age.

"She dyed her hair purple," Tim offered matter-of-factly.

"Thank you, Tim, that's enough," I hissed at my helpful little brother.

Jan was about two metres away from our table taking another order.

"Because she didn't want anyone to recognize her because…"

I leapt round the table and clapped a hand over Leo's mouth while slowly turning round to check Jan hadn't tuned into the conversation. She wouldn't have been too pleased if she'd known that I'd sneaked out of the house to come to the café.

"Are you their sister?" Eel asked me in a strange voice.

I slowly removed my hand from Leo's mouth.

"That's right."

"Only half right," said Leo sulkily.

Eel's eyes lit up. "What do you mean?" he asked quickly.

"She's our half-sister," Tim replied.

"Only she acts like a whole one," Leo

added, still sulkily.

I gave Leo a friendly cuff on the head, grinned at him and said, "Don't be cheeky to your elders and betters."

Eel for the moment seemed happy, though I couldn't for the life of me work out why.

"I think we're just about ready to order now," Mrs Bridge told me.

"Right, fire away," I said, pen poised, at which point three of the boys took me literally, stood up and pretended to shoot me. Everybody laughed about that – even Eel. Even *me*! I saw the pleasure on Eel's mum's face at the sight of her son's innocent amusement. Poor woman, I thought, Eel must be hell to live with. I wondered, briefly, who it was who'd been with Eel on Thursday, as this was clearly his mother.

"Right, Alice, you wanted beefburger, chips and beans, didn't you?"

It took nearly five minutes to get down all the orders. I then copied them on to my proper pad, put the bottom copy on the number board hanging up at the till, and gave the top copy to Kevin in the kitchen. His practised eye scanned the order quickly.

"I'm impressed," he told me a moment later, as I was returning to the lion's den. I was just preening myself, feeling proud because of his compliment when he spoilt it.

"I can actually *read* it!"

"Excellent, Kevin," I retorted. "I didn't know you could read."

"OK, one to you," he said, licking his finger and drawing a one in the air. I disappeared with the sound of sizzling fat and Kevin's chuckles ringing in my ears. The children at the party table were about to explode their party poppers. Eel beckoned me to go over to him.

"You can do my one if you want," he said, handing me his party popper with a big smile.

"No, it's OK, Eel. You do it," I said, returning the big smile.

"My name's Hal," he told me, with that strange intense stare of his. I must have looked puzzled because he added slowly and clearly, "Have you ever heard the name Hal before?" I frowned, trying to think if I had. My frown seemed to make him happy, but I couldn't answer because Kevin announced that the food was ready.

"Party table!" he called out loudly, and as if on cue, twelve poppers exploded, sending wavy coloured fronds shooting up into the air and cascading gently down on other people's heads and all over the table. The other customers in the café either jumped or clapped a hand to their chests as if their hearts had missed a beat from the sudden shock!

The next few minutes were hectic to say the least. I rushed backwards and forwards with beefburgers, fish fingers and chips, and cheesy baked potatoes. The drinks were even more complicated but in the end the chaos subsided and there was a bit of calm while twelve hungry children tucked in appreciatively.

Hal stood out in so many ways. He was the only one without a hat on, the only one with an adult on either side of him, the only one who looked about him and seemed to be weighing things up all the time, and most creepy of all, the only one who appeared to be keeping a constant eye on me. Whenever I went into the kitchen and came back into the café, his frightened eyes filled with relief at my return.

"He's taken a real shine to you, dear," said the lady with Hal as I cleared the plates away a little later.

"Er … yes … he seems to have done," I stammered, wondering what on earth it was with this kid that I couldn't even come straight out with something like, "Are you his mother?" or, "Why is he so weird?" I gave myself a tough telling off for being pathetic as I went to the counter on the pretext of getting more serviettes. While I was at the counter I felt a little tap on my arm and there beside me stood Hal.

"What's your name?" he asked me.

"Lucy."

"Lucy what?" he asked breathlessly.

"Lucy Edmunson."

"Haven't you got a middle name?"

"Oh … right. Lucy Anne Edmunson."

"Are you sure?" he then asked, in an odd voice.

I hesitated because I was trying to work out how his strange little brain was ticking, then I suddenly worked it out. He was obviously confused because Tim and Leo are called Baxter not Edmunson, as Mum remarried, and my stepdad is Terry Baxter.

"The thing is, Hal, the twins and I have got the same mother," I began to explain, "but not the same father. *My* father is married to someone else now but…"

I was about to say, "we all get on well together," when he suddenly snapped, "Oh, shut up, you looked better with your scarf on!" And with that he marched back to his place. I swung round to see what on earth had made him so angry all of a sudden, but it was just as though the conversation with me hadn't existed. He wasn't looking in my direction, he was busy negotiating with his mother to swap places so he could sit next to

Tim. Tim wasn't taking any notice, and Hal's mother was chatting like mad to Mrs Bridge so she swapped places without paying any attention, and carried on gassing happily.

Hal then glanced over at me so I shot my eyes to another table and pretended to be concentrating hard. When I looked back a few seconds later it was to see him surreptitiously exchanging his own nearly full plate for Tim's empty one.

"Come on, slow coach," Mrs Bridge said to Tim. "Everybody else has finished and you've hardly started. We'll be on jellies and ice-cream in a minute, so you need to eat a bit faster."

"But I ate all mine," said Tim protestingly.

"Well, where did this food appear from then? Hmm?" Mrs Bridge asked rather impatiently.

"I don't know, but I ate all mine, so I'm not eating all this as well," Tim said stubbornly, folding his arms in true Tim fashion. Hal, meanwhile, sat beside him, quietly sipping his Coke through a straw.

"Good boy, Hal," whispered his mother, looking at the empty plate in front of her son and giving him a rewarding smile. Hal beamed innocently up at her with the straw still between his lips. As soon as she wasn't looking I saw him dribble the contents of the straw into her lap then quickly walk round to the other side of the table and pretend to be asking one of the quiet little girls if he could try on her hat.

"Ugh!" squealed Hal's mother. "My skirt's all wet. How did that happen?"

I decided not to get involved. It was easier. Instead I looked at my watch and prayed that five-thirty would arrive quickly and they'd all go.

"You don't have to eat it all, Tim," Mrs Bridge was saying, "just a few more mouthfuls. I don't think your mum will be very pleased if we send you home hungry, will she? Look at Leo's nice clean plate. He's eaten all his food up."

Tim had obviously put up with as much as he possibly could of this typical mother-speak.

"I've told you, Mrs Bridge, this is *not* my plate. It's probably Eel's. Yes, I bet he swapped it."

"Did you, Hal?" asked Mrs Bridge in the beginnings of a telling off tone.

"He doesn't normally do things like that," Hal's mother said, jumping to her son's defence and sounding a bit irritated with Mrs Bridge. I decided that this was the moment I should intervene.

"Actually, I'm afraid he *did* swap his own plate with Tim's. I saw him do it."

Hal, who had strolled back to his place, gave me a look which would have annihilated me on the spot if looks could kill.

"I did *not*!" he practically yelled.

"Did *so*," Tim argued.

"Did *never*!" Hal continued.

"That's enough!" shouted Mrs Bridge, which caused a few heads to turn. "It really doesn't matter," she added in a calmer voice. "Would you mind clearing the plates now, er…"

"Lucy," I finished off for her. Then I began

the clearing. I could hear Hal's mother getting very cross with him, and Hal defending himself sulkily.

"That girl's telling lies. She doesn't like me. I can tell," he was saying. "Just because it's her brother," he went on protestingly. "It's not fair, whenever anything bad happens I always get the blame, even when I didn't do anything."

Mrs Bridge had very set lips and so did Hal's mum. The two ladies weren't sure what to say or do any more. Hal's mum got up and started fussing round the girls at the other end of the table, then went off to the loo with three of them.

Ben, whose party it was, began to cry. The crying got worse as Hal started teasing him, calling him Bengley Bridge for some unknown reason, then when Mrs Bridge suggested that this might be a bit cruel, he insisted that it was a big compliment because Bengley Bridge was magic. He knew. His teacher said.

I didn't know what on earth he was talking

about so I decided to try to cheer Ben up by telling him about all the different toppings there were for the ice-cream. He eventually managed a smile as he opted for a mixture of raspberry and chocolate sauce on chocolate and strawberry ice-cream. It sounded revolting, but who cared, at least the child was smiling.

Why are boys so much more difficult than girls? I wondered, as I watched the six little angels at the other end of the table, chatting quietly amongst themselves about their favourite party hats, and playing sweet little games of trying on each other's and saying "one, two, three" then holding up a certain number of fingers to indicate how many points they felt the hat they were currently wearing should score out of ten. At least Mrs Bridge was looking a little happier as I'd managed to cheer up birthday boy a little.

My tray was almost full when a familiar voice beside me said, "How's it going?"

"Oh, Jaimini, hi!" I said. It was lovely to see her friendly face. "Let me just get rid of this lot and serve the puddings, then I'll tell you all about how it's going." I raised my eyes to the ceiling to give her a clue.

"I'll be at the corner table," she said with an understanding smile.

"Puddings coming up in a moment," I said to Mrs Bridge as I staggered off to the kitchen with my loaded tray. I was almost at the swing door when I felt a colossal thud under the tray. I gasped as I realized what had happened. Hal had appeared from nowhere and deliberately and violently shoved his fist under the tray so that the plates and cutlery jumped into the air and my aching arms lost control.

The next second lasted about twenty seconds. I watched in horror as plate after plate crashed to the floor and smashed into smithereens. The whole café came to a standstill. Just about everybody had leapt to their feet and made some sort of shocked or frightened noise. And there we all stood as if paralysed, staring at the most massive breakage mess I've ever seen, which lay scattered on the floor for metres.

It was Jan who broke the spell. Tight-lipped, fast-moving Jan who may as well have been wearing a badge that said, "DON'T WORRY. THIS GIRL WILL BE FIRED." Becky followed in her wake. Even Kevin, who *never* comes out of the kitchen, emerged to look at the wreckage. And into the middle of the silence came his chirrupy observation.

"OK everyone, settle down now. The real entertainment starts in a minute. Lucy here is just the warm-up artist." He then put an arm round my shoulder and gave me a squeeze. The rest of the customers, including all the children, turned back to their tables with little laughs of relief because Kevin had at least lightened the atmosphere. I wished I could have buried my head in his strong shoulder and cried and cried. I wouldn't have cared if I'd got grease and sauce and crumbs from his apron all over me.

"Don't just stand there, Lucy," Jan hissed up at me through gritted teeth. "I hope you realize that this will come out of your wages for the next few sessions if I can put up with you for that long."

"Hey hey, hold on," Kevin interrupted, which is rare for Kevin. "Don't you think we ought to find out what happened first?"

"It's obvious what happened – what *always* happens when Lucy's around," Jan snapped back at him. "Disaster strikes because she lives with her head in the clouds."

"It wasn't my fault. It was that boy," I began to defend myself, almost in tears.

"What boy?" asked Jan, as she, Becky and Kevin all broke off their frantic sweeping and looked round. And that's when he appeared from the loo. He'd obviously nipped in there so nobody could attach any blame to him, the conniving little stoat.

He certainly knew how to make an entrance, this kid. He walked very slowly. Big tears rolled down his face and mingled with … *oh, no, please don't let it be!* … Blood! It was. Did I do that? Did one of those plates hit him? It can't have done. He escaped the moment he had delivered his whacking great clout.

"Oh, my goodness!" cried Hal's mother as she leapt up from the table and came over to the pathetic-looking little boy who had artfully created a scene where he took centre stage once again. Jan practically knocked the mother out of the way, she was so keen to check the boy's injuries. Examining his face carefully, she pulled some tissues from her apron pocket and began dabbing away as he whimpered softly. It certainly looked as though he had been cut quite badly, but I just couldn't understand how. His mother fussed around him with more tissues and I heard Jan ask, "What's your name, pet?"

"Hal," he answered with a little sob.

"How did this happen, Hal? How did you hurt yourself?"

Hal then turned off the tears and the whimpers and faced me with an expression of nothing less than hate.

"*She* did it! She deliberately hurt me because she was cross with me."

"What made you think she was cross with you, pet?"

"Because her brother couldn't eat all his food up, and she tried to blame it on me. She said I'd swapped the plates over, but I hadn't, honestly." Once again the tears welled up in Hal's eyes.

This kid is something else, I thought.

"He's lying," I said to Jan briefly because I'd suddenly had enough of this.

"People always blame me," wailed Hal, "even when I'm telling the truth."

"Perhaps a bit of broken plate caught him on the cheek, and it was nobody's fault," Becky suggested.

"That's impossible," I snapped back at her. "Broken crockery doesn't bounce. Look, I've told you, that kid deliberately came up to me and shoved his fist hard against the bottom of my tray, which is what made me drop it."

"Yes, he did," came Jaimini's soft voice. "He somehow knocked the tray out of Luce's hands."

Half of me was thinking, at long last, I'm about to be believed. Jaimini is a key witness. But the other half was thinking, why is she being so diplomatic about it? Why say that he *somehow knocked* the tray, when it was blatantly obvious he deliberately whacked it.

"But why? Why would he do such a thing?" Hal's mother demanded, sticking up for her son loyally as other customers followed the argument with keen interest, but no other witnesses stepped forward. Thank goodness Jaimini had seen what happened.

"I don't know why," I said crossly, "unless it was because he thought I looked better with my scarf on…" The moment I'd said it, I regretted it. I mean, what a stupid thing to say. Even Jaimini was looking at me as though I was stark, staring mad.

"Oh, don't be ridiculous," Hal's mother said, grabbing her son by the shoulders and marching him back to the table. "We don't have to stand for this." She had a quick word with Mrs Bridge, then put on her coat, helped Hal into his anorak, and left the café without so much as a backward glance at me. Jaimini put a comforting arm round my shoulder as Jan, Becky and Kevin went back into the kitchen.

"Do you want me to help?" Jaimini asked me gently.

"It's OK," was all I could manage to say before I slowly and spiritlessly went out to the kitchen to get the ice-creams and jellies. The rest of the children didn't appear to be at all perturbed by the little drama. They were all chatting happily when I turned up with their desserts.

"I'm sorry about that, Mrs Bridge," I muttered. "I hope things will be better now that that boy has gone." Mrs Bridge patted my arm.

"Don't worry, dear. I didn't actually see what happened, but I've heard that Hal is quite a handful – and I suppose it's not his fault, really."

I started to protest but she patted my arm again. "No, I don't mean what happened just now, I mean his behaviour in general. He's had a tough little life."

I didn't say anything, but neither did I move away, so she continued.

"That lady – Mrs Perry – has just adopted Hal. This afternoon's little episode may have made her think again. Apparently, for some unknown reason, Hal's behaviour has got worse since she and her husband adopted him. While they were just fostering him he wasn't half such a handful. She's not his first foster mother either, Mrs Perry, but she's tough. She'll not be defeated."

"Is he an orphan?" I asked wide-eyed.

"No, not an orphan, but apparently his parents abandoned him when he was only two. They left the country and haven't been traced since."

"Oh, I'd no idea," I stammered. She patted my hand again and I went off thoughtfully to the kitchen.

Jan didn't say another word to me until the last customer had gone and the CLOSED sign was finally on the door. Becky and Kevin had both finished and left. Jaimini was helping me with the last bit of clearing up and washing up. I took my apron off and Jan suddenly delivered the following speech.

"I don't know whose fault that was earlier on, Lucy, and frankly I don't care. All I know is that you and trouble are inseparable. You are the only one out of the six of you girls who is continually causing problems, and I want you to regard this as a final warning. You can forego your wages for today, and I will say no more about it, but…"

At that point I blew a gasket and spoke as I'd never before or since spoken to Jan, in a loud, harsh, sarcastic voice, accompanied by Jaimini's tapping my leg to shut me up. The taps became whacks as my anger took me over.

"Thank you, Jan. Thank you for trusting me. Thank you for believing Jaimini when she told you what happened. Thank you for taking the trouble to find out a bit of background on that weird kid – abandoned at the age of two, two sets of foster parents – isn't exactly the perfect set of circumstances to breed a happy well-adjusted kid, is it? But let's blame Lucy, shall we? Of course, she's going to turn on a kid and smash him in the face with broken crockery, then create a lovely big mess on the floor, isn't she? Because Lucy always gets it wrong, doesn't she? Well, listen Jan, I'll save you the pain and trouble of having to put up with me a moment longer. I'm sure the rest of the girls will understand completely. I quit!"

And with that I stomped out of the café. I was still in a flaring temper half-way down the street when Jaimini caught me up. I didn't know what she'd said to Jan after my dramatic exit, all I could think of was the look on Jan's face. Sheer, unadulterated shock. She had gone quite white and her mouth had dropped open. I didn't think I'd ever managed to shock an adult quite so effectively, so why was I standing there blubbing into Jaimini's hanky, while she herself kept repeating, "Don't worry, Luce, we'll sort it out, don't worry."

Thank goodness the twins couldn't see me in this state. Mum and all the other parents had collected their children at five-thirty. I had made sure I was well out of sight at that time. Goodness only knows what Tim and Leo had told her. I could just imagine their garbled incomprehensible tale… "Luce dropped a tray, Mum…" "Yeah, it was mega!" "You should have seen the tomato ketchup all over the place." "She cut this boy called Eel on the face." "Yeah, but he's a pain and I'm glad she cut him."

I almost started another bout of blubbing at the thought of Mum getting at me when I got home, but Jaimini told me to be quiet and listen to her for a moment.

"Luce, there's lot of heat in this whole episode at the moment, and the most important thing of all to do right now is to let the heat out of it – give it a chance to cool down. I think it's best if you phone your mum and see if you can stay the night with me. If she mentions anything about smashed plates, just make out that the twins must have been exaggerating. You don't even need to go home at all. You can borrow my toothbrush, and my clothes…"

"And a pair of clean knickers in the morning?"

"And a pair of clean knickers in the morning!"

What a friend! I took her advice, and hoped she would be right, that the heat would soon go out of it.

Chapter 4

The next day – Sunday – we all met up at Fen's place because Fen's parents were out for the day and they'd taken Rachel and Emmy (Fen's younger sisters) with them. They were going to take Fen too, but by that time we'd phoned round to find out whose home would be free for a conference for the six of us, and Fen said it would be no problem pleading homework and staying at home on her own.

So that's why at eleven o'clock we were all sitting in Fen's living room, well sprawling more like, because it's somehow more tempting to sprawl when you've got your parents' home to yourself. You can practically imagine that it's your own house.

Fen was being very free with the soda stream and she served up lemonade and ginger ale in her dad's whisky tumblers like it was going out of fashion. She also opened a huge box of chocolates saying her mum wouldn't mind, in fact we'd be doing her a favour because she was trying to lose weight. Fen's mum is actually as wiry as Fen but nobody challenged Fen's comment because we all know women seem to be permanently on diets.

I was the only one who wasn't sprawling. I was sitting like a ramrod because I felt so nervous. Jaimini had arranged the meeting but she hadn't actually told anyone why it was so urgent. She was about to break the news. At least I thought she was, so it came as quite a shock when she suddenly said, "OK everyone, Luce has got something to tell you all."

"Um," I gulped. "Umm…"

"Well, that's jolly interesting," Andy said and everybody laughed.

"Go on, Luce," Jaimini encouraged me.

Five pairs of eyes were on me.

"Um … I got mad at Jan you see…"

"Why?"

"Because she got mad at me…"

"Why?"

"Because I dropped a tray."

"A tray!"

"Full of plates … and they all smashed – everywhere."

"Oh, Luce!" they breathed.

"Right, I think I'll tell you myself," Jaimini said, sounding just a little irritated. I suppose she had good reason. After all I had told them the story completely the wrong way round with no explanation at all. Fen looked as though she was in a competition to see who could hold their breath the longest. I've never seen anyone waiting so intently to hear something.

"As you know, there was a children's party at the café yesterday," Jaimini began. "At the party there was one rather difficult boy called Hal. It was the same kid that was in the café the other day, the one with the fascination for Luce."

"Crush, it's called," Tash said with a smile.

"No … no, this doesn't seem to be a crush, exactly," Jaimini went on. "The boy was as nice as pie one minute, and the next he suddenly went berserk. Luce was just going to the kitchen with her tray piled sky high, and this kid came along and somehow knocked into Luce and sent all the plates and everything flying, then he bolted off to the loo. A minute later while everyone was standing around staring at the wreckage, he emerged from the loo and stood there with blood on his face, just as though he'd been cut."

"*Had* he been cut?" Fen asked wide-eyed.

"We don't think so," Jaimini answered.

"But you're not certain?" Leah asked.

"No, not totally certain," replied Jaimini. "The point is that Jan is insisting that this is another of…" Jaimini stopped mid-sentence as she realized what she was about to say.

"Go on, say it," I said despondently, "another of Luce's unfortunate accidents."

Jaimini nodded and the others looked down. Fen bit her lip.

"So what was the outcome of all this?" she asked quietly, probably dreading the answer. Jaimini and I looked at each other. This was the hard bit because I had put everybody else's job in jeopardy with my impulsive behaviour. It was also even harder because the way Jaimini had related the story she hadn't made it clear that I wasn't in the wrong.

"Well, you see…" I tried.

"Jan gave Luce a final warning," Jaimini told the other four.

Fen had no sooner heaved a sigh of relief that it wasn't quite as bad as she thought it was going to be, then she gasped in horror at Jaimini's next words.

"…only Luce got mad, and said, 'Don't worry, I'm going anyway!'"

"Oh, Luce! No!" said Tash.

"Why, Luce?" Andy wanted to know.

"Because I was furious, that's why."

"You mean you were furious with yourself?" Leah asked gently.

"No, of course not!" I practically yelled

back at her. "Why should I be furious with myself?"

"Because of dropping the tray," Leah answered quietly.

"But it wasn't my fault," I screeched in frustration.

There was a small pause. All their eyes were down and there suddenly seemed to be an awful lot of fidgeting. I looked from one to another of my friends in amazement as realization dawned on me. They didn't believe me! And why not? It was obvious why not. Because Jaimini hadn't really stuck up for me. My eyes rested last of all on her.

"Tell them, Jaimini! For goodness' sake, tell them how it wasn't my fault!"

"I … I … can't," stammered Jaimini.

"What do you mean, you can't?"

"I didn't actually see what happened…"

"You didn't see!"

"No, I was looking out of the window at the time. All I saw was you standing in the middle of tons of broken crockery, and looking horrified."

"But I told you what happened... I wouldn't lie about it, would I?"

"No ... no ... but..."

"But – what?"

She looked so embarrassed. They all did. I could feel my heart beating against my ribs. They were somehow shutting me out.

"I think Jaimes thinks you've been exaggerating a bit," Andy volunteered.

"Well, I *wasn't* exaggerating," I exploded. "That kid has got a serious problem. I don't know what it is, except that in some weird way, it's got something to do with me. It makes me sick that you don't believe me. You're supposed to be my friends. And as for you...!" I turned on Jaimini as my temper hit the roof – "I thought you were supposed to be my *best* friend."

"I *am*," she said uncomfortably.

"So why didn't you stick up for me?"

"I did."

"But you don't believe me?"

"It's just that..."

"...it all seems so unlikely," Fen finished

off for her.

"Well, now there are five of you," I said, getting up and making for the door. "I hope the rota works without me. I hope *everything* works without me!"

I left the room and went out of Fen's front door, leaving five former friends and a stunned silence behind me. My walk home was one of the loneliest walks I have ever had. My eyes kept welling up with tears. I couldn't understand why none of them believed me. I knew I was prone to exaggerate, but surely they realized I wouldn't exaggerate about something as big as this.

I crept in quietly through our back door so that I could splash cold water over my face before I had to see any of my family. No such luck. Mum was in the kitchen.

"Hello, Lucy. Did you have a nice time?" I nodded and tried to look normal. "You're very glassy-eyed, love. That's usually a sign of a temperature. Here." And she whipped a thermometer out of the kitchen medicine cabinet.

I sat down at the table and pretended to read the newspaper while my temperature was being taken, but really I was reading the same sentence over and over again without taking it in, because my mind couldn't stop playing and replaying the horrible conversation that had taken place at Fen's house. The more I thought about it the more miserable I felt, and the crosser I felt with the nauseating little brat who had landed me in all this trouble.

"Perfectly normal," said Mum, after tilting the thermometer this way and that to try and read the mercury level. "I'm surprised because you look as though you've got a temperature."

"I feel fine," I said. "I'm just going to finish off some homework."

"OK," she answered cheerfully, without noticing my downcast look as I turned and trudged upstairs. Once in my room with the door shut, I lay down on my bed and stared up at the ceiling thinking what on earth to do.

I couldn't go to school the next day. The rest of the girls wouldn't want to talk to me after my dramatic exit – my second one of the weekend. Perhaps I could say I was ill again. Yes, I could smuggle the thermometer out of the kitchen, hold it under the hot tap for a while then show it to Mum when the mercury level had risen well above normal. It would be no problem getting three or four days off school. Just until… Until what? I thought. Jaimini's words came back to me – "until the heat has gone out of it."

So that was her clever little plan. She just wanted me to calm down a bit then presumably she thought that I'd admit I *had* been exaggerating, then we could all sit down and discuss sensibly how I was going to go crawling back to Jan, humbly apologizing and begging her to let me come back to work at the café.

Jaimini and the others obviously cared more about their stupid jobs than they did about me. I turned over and sobbed into the pillow for about a minute as I realized that it was no good having a few days off school. It would only be putting off the moment when I would have to face the problem. Or would it?

I sat up slowly as the obvious perfect solution entered my head. I would go and live with Dad. I wouldn't phone. I'd just go, then he couldn't turn me away. I'd phone Mum when I got there so she wouldn't send out any search parties. I looked at my watch. Twelve-thirty. The next train to Perrington, where Dad lives, would be at one-thirty. I somehow had to get myself to the station at Limendowling which was about five miles from Cableden. I'd need to get a lift from someone.

Obviously I couldn't ask Mum or Terry, my stepdad, because the whole trip was top secret. I didn't want any well-meaning person to try and stop me escaping. So that meant that all adults were out of the question. It would all seem very mysterious and odd to them. There was nothing for it, I would have to hitch a lift. Mum would be furious if she ever found out but with any luck that wouldn't happen.

I packed a small bag with nothing but the basics. I was tempted to put all sorts of trendy tops and things in there, but I knew I had to be ruthless and just pack the minimum.

My heart was in my mouth as I crept downstairs with my bag and coat. I paused halfway to listen. The twins were watching a video and it sounded like Mum was still in the kitchen. Terry was obviously in there too because I could hear both their voices. I tiptoed quickly and quietly down the last few stairs and out of the front door, clicking it shut as gently as I could.

Once outside I ran as fast as possible with my heavy bag thumping me on the hip-bone with every step I took. I felt safer when I'd turned the corner and was no longer in view from any window of our house. I felt safer but no calmer. I just wanted to be on that train then nobody could stop me getting to Dad's.

Right, now to stick my thumb out. I hesitated for ages because I'd been told and told countless times about the dangers of hitching lifts. A little argument was going on inside my head … "Go on Lucy, get on with it." "No Lucy, it's too dangerous." "You'll be

OK." "It's not worth the risk." "Yes it is. You've got to get to that station and on to that train before anyone stops you."

I had been rushing along with my thoughts, looking at the pavement, but I suddenly looked up and thank goodness I did, because there in the distance, but rapidly approaching me, were Andy and Leah. I did not want to be seen by any of my so-called friends at this moment in time, but short of turning round and walking in the opposite direction there was absolutely nothing I could do. No convenient little side roads I could slip along, no handy bus shelters I could hide inside.

As luck would have it though, there was a car parked on the other side of the road. If I ran across the road quickly I could duck down behind that car before they realized it was me. Right! Action! Look right, look left, look right again… Hang on a sec. I recognize that car coming towards me. I recognize that driver. Kevin was pulling up beside me. He rolled down the window.

"Do you and that heavy bag want a lift

anywhere?" he asked in his usual friendly voice. "I'm going to Limendowling."

"Yes, please, Kevin." I bundled myself and my bag in his car before you could say "knife", and as he pulled away from the kerb I pretended that I'd dropped a coin from my pocket, and bent right over, my head down under the dashboard, pretending to grovel about on the floor for it.

"Isn't that Andy and Leah?" Kevin said, as I prayed he wouldn't stop.

"'Spect so. They're going to… Oh, where *is* that coin?"

I stayed down there till I was quite certain we'd be past Andy and Leah, then I came back up again. I'd judged it perfectly. I sat back in the seat with a contented sigh. At last I was really getting away.

"Running away, are you?" asked Kevin, like a mind-reader.

"No!" I answered, a little too protestingly.

"Only joking," he laughed.

"Oh, yes, right." I managed my own thin little laugh. "I'm going to see my dad. Just for the afternoon, you know."

"Where does he live?"

"Oh, near the station," I lied because obviously I couldn't tell him where Dad really lived or he'd realize I couldn't possibly be going there and back all in one afternoon, and then he'd get suspicious because of school and everything. As far as I knew, Kevin had no idea that I'd yelled at Jan and told her where to put her job, and I didn't want to discuss anything about the café because that was dangerous territory for me.

"What's in the bag?" he suddenly asked me.

Another difficult one to answer. I could hardly say "enough clothes to last me at least a week."

"Some old toys and books that the boys have grown out of. They're for Colette and Edward – my dad's little children."

"It's quite a big tribe you've got, isn't it?" Kevin remarked chattily.

"Yes, it can be complicated at times," I agreed, trying not to sound as though I was forcing the conversation, which I was.

"Are you all right, Lucy?" Kevin asked out of the blue, turning to me with concern all over his face. "Only you don't seem yourself."

"No, I'm fine," I answered in a bright voice. "I always get like this when I'm going to see Sally. She's my dad's new wife and she and Mum don't get on, you see."

"Oh, yeah, families, eh? Who'd have 'em?" He gave me a sympathetic shrug obviously completely taken in by that quickly improvised excuse for my tense behaviour. We drove in silence for a while then he asked where exactly I wanted to be dropped off.

"Oh, at the station'll be fine," I said lightly.

"Don't be daft, I'll drop you at the door. There's no need to lug that great bag any further than necessary." He frowned. "Hang on a sec. What would you have done if I hadn't turned up?"

"Er … I was going to ask Andy's dad because he had a train to catch this afternoon."

"Oh yeah, right," said Kevin, who had no idea that I'd be more likely to charter a plane than go in a car with Andy's dad.

"Tell me where to stop." We had arrived at the station. I saw a tall good-looking boy standing just by the entrance to the car park. I'd never set eyes on him before in my life, but decided he'd do fine. "Oh, there's Robert Goodwin," I said, quickly inventing a name for him. "I'll just go and say 'Hi'. Thanks a million for the lift, Kevin. See you sometime."

"Yeah, OK. See you." He winked at me as I got out of the car. "Good-looking lad, that!"

I blushed, which was quite convenient because it looked as though that was why I'd asked to be dropped at the station and not outside my dad's, because I was secretly meeting a boy and not going to my dad's at all.

I strolled as slowly as I could up to the tall, good-looking "Robert", praying that Kevin would drive off quickly. He seemed to be taking his time so I turned round and gave him a bright little wave, then pretended to drop another coin. He must have thought I was becoming amazingly clumsy! As I straightened up I heard his car pull away.

"Thank goodness for that," I said to myself as I walked past the boy and into the station waiting room to buy my ticket. The one way ticket to Perrington cost me nearly all the money I'd got. Never mind, it was worth it. The train was bang on time. I got into the carriage with two other people and for the first time for ages, I actually managed to relax enough to read my book. There were six stations before Perrington, but the time flew by and hardly anybody seemed to get on or off the train except at Perrington itself which was quite a big town.

I handed my ticket in and decided to phone Dad from the station because I couldn't face the walk which was about twenty-five minutes, or probably more with a heavy bag to carry.

Standing in the telephone kiosk my spirits once again began to sink as ring after ring came and went and nobody answered. At the end of eighteen rings I reluctantly replaced the receiver and decided I'd have to walk. It wasn't an enjoyable walk because I knew what lay at the other end of it – a wait, and possibly a long one. I started wondering where Dad and Sally and the kids may have gone and what time they might be back. Colette and Edward were still quite little so they'd need to get to bed fairly early.

It was no good. No matter how much I tried to cheer myself up as I trudged along, I knew in my heart that things were not going as I had planned. The awful, lonely feeling started creeping round me again.

I waited for two hours on Dad's back doorstep. I didn't stay there all the time. I kept getting up and walking round the garden. I searched under slabs and pots and in every conceivable hiding place for a key to the house or even to the garden shed, but no luck.

As I grew colder and colder and my hands started to turn mottled blue I tried not to cry at the hopelessness of everything. I was sitting, shoulders hunched, arms hugging myself, rocking backwards and forwards when I heard a wonderful sound – the sound of a car pulling up outside the house.

I didn't want to go rushing out to the front until I was sure it was Dad and Sally, so I listened intently, waiting for the sound of little children's voices. A door slammed. I could hear footsteps, just one set of footsteps and no voices. The footsteps were getting louder. Whoever it was, was definitely coming round the back. I had a moment of fear because the way my luck was going, this was probably a burglar who would attack me first, then burgle Dad's house.

My eyes must have looked like saucers as I stared at the corner of the house, where someone was about to appear.

"Hello, love," he said softly.

"Hello, Terry," I whispered. Then I hurled myself at him, buried my head in his woolly sweater and burst into tears.

"It's OK, love," he kept whispering, and I thought how lucky I was to have such a brilliant stepfather who knew where to find me, who came to get me and who held me tight without asking any questions.

"S-sorry," I stammered.

"You're freezing," he answered. "Come on, the car's lovely and hot. I've been burning rubber!"

So we walked round to the car and talked. "Why burning rubber?" I asked.

"I was in a hurry to get my girl back. You left me alone with those two monsters."

"What about Mum?"

"She's looking after the monsters. We guessed you'd be here."

"But how? I didn't leave any clues."

"Kevin popped round to see us."

"Kevin! Why?"

"Because he was worried about you."

"But I told Kevin my dad lived at Limendowling and I'm sure he believed me..."

"He believed you until you said you were going to say 'Hi' to a boy called Robert, because the boy's name is actually Mick... You see, as it happened, Kevin knew that boy, so he immediately realized something was wrong. At first he didn't think anything of it, but then he drove back a moment later and saw you in the station waiting room. He didn't feel that he could stop you, but he decided that he ought to let us know. And thank goodness he did."

"Oh," I answered because there was really nothing more to be said.

We drove along in silence for a while then Terry suddenly said, "What's the matter, Lucy? What's so bad in your life that you felt you had to escape to your dad's?"

"It's too complicated to explain," I answered, "and nobody else believes me, so why should you?"

"Try me."

So I did. I told from start to finish about the weird kid, then about the fact that I'd yelled at Jan but I asked him not to tell Mum about that. And finally about the fact that I wouldn't be working at the café any more.

"Do you regret that?" he asked.

I nodded.

"Well, why not try to talk to Jan more reasonably now the heat's gone out of it all."

"You sound just like Jaimini."

"She's the brainy one, isn't she?"

"That's right."

"Oh, good. Glad I'm in good company," he grinned.

"You believe me about Hal, don't you, Terry?"

There was the briefest of pauses.

"Y… yes," he answered.

The pause said it all. I felt the anger rising again. Everybody was sorry for me, everybody was rooting for me, but nobody actually believed me. Right, I would get hold of that kid. Somehow I would track him down and get a public apology out of him. I wasn't going to allow an eight-year-old boy to make me look a fool.

For the rest of the journey home Terry and I didn't say much. I expect he was being diplomatic – and as for me, I was plotting. I was wondering whether or not to go back to plan A and try to get some more time off school – say I'd had a relapse or something. It would be understandable after all that time sitting about in the freezing cold.

Mum welcomed me like a long-lost stranger. "Oh, Lucy, if only you'd told me you wanted to see your dad, I would have arranged it, love. Only, this weekend they're visiting Sally's parents in Winchester. They won't be back till tomorrow morning."

"I didn't specially want to see Dad. I just wanted to get away for a bit."

"I'll explain, Melanie," said Terry to my mum, who was looking very worried, and no doubt wondering how she'd failed me, which of course she hadn't.

"Well, the phone hasn't stopped ringing since you went. All your friends phoned."

"What did they want?" I asked, a bit aggressively.

"Well, Tash phoned first and said she was sorry if she or any of the girls had upset you. They didn't mean to."

Typical Tash – the peacemaker, but like I said, I don't want people feeling sorry for me.

"Then Fen phoned, then Leah, then Andy. They all asked where you were. I said I didn't know, but I was sure you'd turn up soon.

94

They said they'd see you at school tomorrow."

Huh! Not even sorry, just "see you at school". Well, not if I could help it they wouldn't.

"Oh, and Jaimini came round."

"What did she want?" I asked.

"She wanted to talk to you. She seemed really upset. She asked me to get you to phone her the moment you got in."

"I'm going to bed," I said to Mum. "I don't feel too good."

Mum sighed as I wearily climbed the last few stairs. "Night," she said gently.

"Night," I replied. But I doubt she heard.

Chapter 5

The next day I woke up with a new feeling of determination in me. I *would* go to school. I would be polite but distant to the other five. When they were ready to believe me, I would be friends, but until then they would have to whistle for it. I got to school at the latest possible moment to avoid having to see any of them before assembly.

It was at morning break that Tash came to find me.

"Luce," she began a little shakily, "I really want us all to be friends."

"I can't be friends until you believe me," I replied firmly. Then she asked me if I'd go with her to talk to the rest of the girls. She said there was something important they wanted to discuss.

Tash and I walked down to the netball courts in silence, because neither of us knew what to say. The others were already there when we arrived. All except Jaimini who was off school ill. She'd probably got what I'd had, or maybe, like me, she couldn't face coming to school when there was such a bad atmosphere.

I had wondered on the way whether or not the girls were going to apologize, but I had to admit, they certainly didn't look on first sight as though they were about to apologize. They looked more as though they were going to break some bad news. This was not far from the truth.

Andy was looking the most anxious of them all. It was she who spoke first.

"The thing is, Luce, now you've dropped out of the café rota, it's left us with big problems. You see, my dad's come home. He's got three weeks' leave. That means I can't possibly work at the café in case he turns up there. It's supposed to be me on duty though, and nobody else is free…"

"Why not?" I interrupted.

"Well, I've had my violin lesson time altered," Leah said softly. "And Jaimini's ill."

"What about you?" I asked Fen.

"Tash and I have signed up for that dance club. It's by audition only, and the auditions are today after school."

"Well, I don't see why I should do it," I said, a bit crossly. "I've already told you, until I get an apology from Jan I'm not going back to work. I'd have to apologize to *her* if I wanted to go to work today, and that would be like admitting that I dropped the tray by accident, and whatever you lot think, *I did not!*"

"Wouldn't it be better to apologize to Jan than risk losing your job?" Fen said, rather impatiently.

I was about to snap back at her when Andy intervened.

"Oh, Luce, couldn't you please just do it

this once, *only* this once … *please*," she said, looking desperate.

"The chances of your dad strolling through Cableden and seeing you through the café window are pretty remote, aren't they?" I pointed out.

"I suppose so, but honestly Luce, I just daren't risk it. If he caught me it would be so awful – and for Mum as well, because he'd realize we'd been lying to him."

"Can't you say you've got a netball practice after school?"

"But I've already said I'll come straight home after school…"

"Yes, but you could say that a match had been arranged at the last minute – or say they've started a gym club or something and you forgot to mention it."

"That's when Dad would get suspicious. If I don't turn up at home at the normal time, he'll come and investigate, and if I phone and say I'll be late, he'll come and meet me, and I won't be there. I don't want a repetition of what happened last time."

"That was awful, wasn't it?" Fen said. Fen had had to phone Andy at the café and warn her that her dad was going to meet her at the school. But she had to say it all in code because Andy's dad was in the same room as her at the time. She told us all about it afterwards and it beat anything I've ever seen on television.

"I'm not going through that again," Andy said, shivering involuntarily.

All through this I had been wondering what on earth to do, but in the end I thought it wasn't fair because no one was prepared to believe me and everybody thought I could give up my principles when they weren't prepared to give up their clubs and things. I really didn't think I was being any more selfish than the rest of them.

"None of you stood by me after the Hal episode and now you expect me to forget all about that and carry on as though it never happened. Well, I can't. I'm sorry."

With that I got up and left. As I walked away I heard Andy say, "She's right, you know. We didn't stick by her. I'll just have to get on with it and start praying."

I couldn't hear any reply if there was one. A part of me felt stubborn and proud because Andy was obviously really afraid of her dad, but the other part of me was saying, "No, Luce, stick to your guns, don't let them walk all over you."

I spent the rest of the day forming plans while trying to avoid the other four. I felt lonely and sad and it was tempting at times to try and forget the whole "Hal" thing, just to get back to how I used to be with my friends. I even considered apologizing humbly to Jan, but only for a fleeting moment, before a picture of that nauseating kid shoving his fist under my tray came into my head, and made me determined to track him down and get an explanation and an apology out of him.

I decided to skip the last twenty minutes of school and go and corner him at the primary school where he and my brothers all went. I didn't know why on earth I hadn't thought of that before. It was so obvious. I would try and get to him before his mother did.

The last lesson was geography and Mr Butler didn't make a murmur when I said I had an orthodontist appointment. So I strolled out of school looking pretty confident. If you look in any way unsure of yourself it gives you a furtive look and that makes teachers suspicious. I learnt that ages ago.

As I approached the twins' school I found myself deep in thought about Andy's dad. I'd only ever seen him once and he certainly looked scary. He's tall and dark with very sallow skin and hooded eyelids. He doesn't smile much and he's often sarcastic. He's extremely strict about everything. When Andy's mum first mentioned the café to him he said, "Categorically *no*. Under no circumstances will my thirteen-year-old daughter work in a café."

Mrs Sorrell, Andy's mum, thinks that she can gradually get him used to the idea, but it obviously hasn't happened yet, otherwise Andy wouldn't have been the nervous wreck she was today.

As I rounded the bend in the road just before the twins' primary school I heard the end of school bell go. I hurried the last few metres and had a look round at the parents who were waiting at the school gate. Quite a few were sitting in their cars but I couldn't see Mrs Perry amongst them, and nor was she one of the ones at the gate.

Just then I caught sight of Tim. "Hi," I called out, running into the school grounds to meet him.

"What are you doing here, Lucy?" he called out in a big showy-offy voice for the benefit of his friends. Tim and Leo often walked home on their own because our house was so close. Sometimes Mum collected them, but I never did.

"Where's Hal?" I whispered to Tim.

"Where's Eel?" Tim demanded loudly of no one in particular. "Oh, there he is," he added, pointing at the skinny figure of Hal heading towards the school gate.

"Hal," I called out as I hurried over to him. He took one look at me and bolted, but I'm quite a fast runner and I managed to stop him by grabbing hold of his bag.

"Get off," he said trying to squirm out of my grasp because by then I had got hold of his arm.

"Not until you give me an explanation for what you did in the café on Saturday afternoon," I said, aggressively.

"Let go of me. You're hurting me," he said in a loud whine, and when I didn't he added, "I'll tell the teacher."

I then propelled him with one arm behind his back towards the school gate to get him out of calling distance of any teachers. That was my big mistake because Hal screamed at the top of his voice, "Help! Help! I'm being kidnapped!"

"Don't be ridiculous, I'm not kidnapping you," I started to say, but the damage was done. In seconds I became surrounded by four women. The last to arrive was a teacher, who demanded angrily, "What's happening? What are you trying to do with Hal?"

Hal began his famous whimpering as I

hung my head and said, "I wasn't taking him anywhere."

"It looked like you were to me," said one of the helpful parents.

"She 'ad 'im in an armlock," offered another one of them.

And at that point Mrs Perry appeared on the scene.

"Not you again," she said, looking at me rather fiercely.

"Has this young lady been a problem to you before?" the enthusiastic teacher wanted to know. And that's when Mum arrived.

"Lucy! What are you doing here?"

"Abducting little boys," one of the parents answered rudely which made Mum turn white.

"I came to try and get to the bottom of why Hal is behaving as he is towards me," I told Mum softly and as calmly as I could. I was well aware of all the parents and children standing around enjoying the scene. Tim and Leo had long since disappeared, probably feeling terribly embarrassed.

"I know my daughter," Mum said, putting a protective arm round my shoulder, "and she wouldn't harm or hurt anyone. Don't worry, Miss Watkins, I'll sort it out from here. I'm sorry, Mrs Perry, for any upset Lucy may have caused."

And with that smooth little speech Mum had managed to pacify the overzealous Miss Watkins, taken the wind out of the other parents' sails and reduced them to a state of tutting and sighing as they wandered away, probably disappointed that there hadn't been a more dramatic ending to the episode. Some people are like that – never happy unless they're watching someone else in big trouble.

Trotting along beside Mum, I felt like a six-year-old who'd pinched another child's tube of Smarties and eaten them all. Mum didn't say anything till we got home, then she sat me down in the kitchen and insisted that I start at the beginning and tell her the whole Hal story from my point of view, even though Terry had already explained it all once. When I'd finished, she didn't really know what to say, because just like everyone else, she obviously didn't believe me. She thought I was exaggerating but she felt quite sorry for me – same old story.

I stared out of the window feeling wretched and upset. And that's when I saw something that made my heart miss a beat, if not two. Strolling down our road towards town was Andy's dad. *Omigod!* Was he going to the café?

For about ten seconds I stayed stock still while loads of different thoughts and ideas bumped into each other inside my head, and finally all of them disappeared leaving one big thought on its own. *I have to get to the café.*

Without further ado I crept out of the front door, stopping only to grab Terry's golfing umbrella which was huge and very brightly coloured. Then I ran down the road after Andy's dad. As I got nearer to him, I slowed down ready for the disguise to be put in place and the overtaking procedure to be put into action. I put the big bright brolly up with a flourish, and lowered it so it covered the whole of my head as well as the top of my shoulders.

It wasn't easy to walk because I could only just see through it. I didn't care what I looked like, I just needed to get past him. This I managed, though how I didn't poke him in the eye, I'll never know. I could have sworn he did a short laugh, but it couldn't have been, because Andy's dad never laughs at anything.

Once safely past him I began to run until I'd rounded a bend in the road, then I put the umbrella down and got my breath a bit before putting on another spurt.

When at last I got to the café I was exhausted, and felt really stupid going in there with a huge umbrella when it wasn't even raining. There was a hat stand just inside the café so I hung the umbrella up there and went to sit down.

The first person I saw when I sat down at the corner table was Andy. Her eyes looked coal-black and enormous, set in a pale pinched face. She was so preoccupied she didn't even notice me. She just disappeared into the kitchen.

I ordered a Coke from Mark and sat there sipping it very slowly with my eyes on the door. After ten minutes when nobody apart from three elderly ladies had come in, I began to relax. Andy's dad was obviously going somewhere else. We were all probably getting a bit neurotic about him. Andy hadn't emerged at all from the kitchen. Jan was buzzing about and either hadn't noticed me or, more likely, was deliberately ignoring me.

On a sudden hunch I decided to go and investigate the men's toilets and see if young Hal had left any clues lying around. It had occurred to me that I had never got to the bottom of that blood on his face, and I was convinced it was fake blood that he'd subtly administered in the loo. After all, come to think about it, there was absolutely no sign of any mark or scar on his face when I saw him at school.

Getting into the gents when you're not a gent has to be a well-timed procedure. I was lucky. There were no men or boys in the café at that time, so I could relax and take my time. This I did, peering into corners, standing on tiptoe to run my finger along the high window ledge, but there was not a scrap of evidence. Then my eyes alighted on the waste paper basket and I felt a ray of hope. There was only one thing in that bin and it was a very slim bottle with the tiniest trace of red in the bottom of it. I read the label – FAKE BLOOD. Just as I had thought. Eureka! I pocketed the bottle and went out. Opening the door, who should I come face to face with but Andy's dad!

"Hello, Mr Sorrell," I gulped.

"Young Lucy Edmunson, isn't it?"

"Y-yes."

"Interesting place to meet," he commented with eyebrows raised and a tiny jerk of the head at the words GENTS written as clearly as anything on the door.

"I … I was … taking the opportunity to check there was enough loo paper in there… I … I work here, you see."

"So I hear."

With that he gave me a dismissive look as if to say, "I don't talk to girls who work in cafés, so out of my way, skivvy," then he pushed open the door to the gents and went in. Once again I could have sworn I heard a little titter come from him. Perhaps it was a smirk.

I zoomed straight to the kitchen where Andy was washing up with shoulders hunched. Jan was in the café.

"Oh, Luce, he's here. I've seen him…"

Without further ado I whipped the apron off her and said, "I'm taking your place. Get going quick while he's in the loo…"

"What about Jan?"

"That's my problem."

"Luce, I can't thank you enough."

"Buzz off quick. I'll tell your dad you're buying some earrings for Jaimini, so go and hover about near the jeweller's, OK?"

"OK."

And she was gone, leaving me with a massive dilemma. Kevin had been carefully placing cakes and gateaux in the freezer, and when he turned round it was to see that a transformation had taken place – the washer-upper had changed from Andy Sorrell to Lucy Edmunson.

"I must be going mad!" he joked. "I could have sworn that was Andy washing up a moment ago!"

"Andy's dad turned up, so she had to go. Don't say anything to Jan. She's going to flip when she sees me here, without adding to the problem by mentioning Andy's dad."

At that moment Jan walked in. She went straight to the surface where Kevin puts his orders and picked up the food for table ten without even glancing in my direction. Then out she went with her loaded tray.

I was about to breathe out when she came straight back in. This time she went to the big store cupboard. With her back to me she said, "Andy, when you've finished that, could you stock up the fridge in the café with whatever it's short of."

"OK," I answered in a voice which was supposed to sound like Andy's but came out sounding like a frog with flu. Jan immediately whipped round and saw that it was me wearing the apron.

"What's going on?" she asked in a raised voice. "Is this your idea of a joke? I thought better of Andy."

"She's … she's ill," I improvised.

"Well, where is she?" Jan demanded.

"She's … she's in the loo… Being sick."

Kevin did a long low whistle practically under his breath, but I heard it OK. All the same he carried on working. Kevin rarely got involved with anything. Jan said not a word, just stormed back into the café carrying a few cans of Coke. As the door swung hard back I caught a glimpse of Andy's dad back at his table. Jan was heading for the fridge and not the toilets as I had feared she might. I took the opportunity to dive into the ladies. I had just got inside one of the two loos when there was a knock at the door and Jan's voice said, "Andy, are you all right?"

"Yes, thanks," I replied, and this time the voice was much more convincing because I had bunched up my jumper and practically stuffed it into my mouth, which gave a muffled, shaky effect. "Do you mind if Lucy finishes off for me just this once, Jan?"

I held my breath and waited. The weak, shaky voice obviously did the trick. Jan felt sorry for poor, sick Andy, and knew she couldn't manage without an extra pair of hands. "All right Andy, just this once."

As soon as I'd heard that she'd gone, I pulled my jumper back into shape, counted to twenty, then went out of the toilet.

"Lucy, I've been looking for you," Jan said as I entered the café.

"I was checking on Andy."

"Well, she's obviously in a bad way. Do you want to finish off her duty for her?"

I nodded because I couldn't bring myself to say, "Yes, please," because, let's face it, I was doing *her* a favour, not the other way round. Mr Sorrell was sipping tea and I knew I had to speak to him, so as soon as Jan had gone back into the kitchen I approached his table.

"Excuse me, Mr Sorrell, but I thought you might like to know that Andy said she was going to help Jaimini find some earrings after school. So she might be in the jeweller's next door."

Mr Sorrell gave me a curt nod, which I suppose was his own sweet way of saying "Thanks for the info," then he gulped his tea, left some change on the table and briskly left the café. Good riddance! I thought.

I looked at my watch. Good, time seemed to be moving along quite fast. I'd keep a low profile until it was time to go, by staying in the kitchen as much as possible. But first I thought I'd better restock the fridge, which I'd already been asked to do.

A few moments later Jan approached me, looking very concerned. "Is Andy still in the loo?" she asked.

"No, she's gone home. She was feeling too awful even to say goodbye. She looked deathly pale."

"Well, I didn't think she looked very well when she first arrived. I wondered at the time whether or not she'd cope... Oh, *no*!"

"What?"

I turned to see what had alarmed Jan. My heart sank. It was Hal and his mother heading towards one of the central tables.

"Time for me to disappear I think," I murmured. But before I could make my escape, Hal's voice rang out loud and clear, "Oh, no! Look Mum, it's that awful girl who tried to take me away from school today. I'm not staying here with her around. She might try it again. I don't feel safe. Let's go quickly."

Everybody in the café – and it was pretty full – stopped their conversations and turned round to see who the awful girl was. I have never felt so embarrassed, helpless and angry all rolled into one, as I did at that moment. Two women got up looking very flustered and bundled their small children into their buggies, while the third one at the table hurriedly wrote a cheque and they all disappeared in about ten seconds flat.

Hal and Mrs Perry then hurried out and Jan practically pushed me into the kitchen. From the other side of the swing door I could clearly hear her addressing the remaining customers in the café. "Please don't worry, everybody. There must be some mistake. That little boy has obviously mixed Lucy up with someone else."

Kevin suddenly seemed like the only friendly person in a harsh, cruel world. Standing at his side, I heard the buzz of conversation resume, as Jan came into the kitchen.

"What's that all about?" she asked me, in a dangerously cold voice.

"I went to his school to try to get him to confess," I said in a flat voice. There was no spark left in me. I was fighting a losing battle. Everywhere I turned there was hostility, people who didn't trust me, people who didn't believe me, and at the centre of it all was a totally unapproachable boy who was ruining my life. What a mess.

"You are such a thoughtless and impulsive child," Jan snapped. "You are also directly responsible for losing me three of my best customers, Lucy. Take your apron off and get off home. I'd rather manage without you. That poor little boy…"

"He's not a poor little boy. He's a weird kid who's got it in for me."

"You must have a persecution complex or something," Jan shot back at me. "Either that or an imagination that needs severely curbing."

She didn't look at me as I took the apron off, tears welling up in my eyes. "I'll have a chat with her," Kevin whispered to me, giving me a friendly nudge and a wink, but his kindness only made my tears start flowing and then I couldn't speak properly to say thank you, so I just went quietly out of the door, wishing a big hole would appear in the ground and swallow me up for ever.

When I got home I noticed a tiny parcel on the front doorstep. "Luce the Greatest" it said on the front. I opened it to find a sweet little dark blue box inside, and inside that was the loveliest pair of Yin Yang earrings I'd ever seen. There was also a little note which said, "Loads of love, Andy." I smiled and realized that that was the first time I'd smiled in ages.

Mum obviously hadn't even noticed my absence because when we were all sitting round the table tucking into baked potatoes with tuna sauce, she suddenly said, "Oh, those are beautiful earrings, Luce."

"Present from Andy," I told her, feeling happy that she was in a good mood and that I wasn't going to get an earful for going out without saying anything.

"What for?" Leo said. "It ain't your birthday."

"It *isn't* your birthday," Terry corrected him.

"I know, and it ain't Luce's, neither."

"It ain't Luce's *either*," Mum corrected him.

We all laughed at that, because Mum had sounded so funny saying "ain't" by mistake.

Not just a smile, but a *laugh*! I thought. Things are looking up!

Chapter 6

The next day Andy met me as I went into school. She gave me a big hug and told me how nice the earrings looked when I thanked her for them.

"I've been thinking, Luce," she said. "You've helped me, and now I want to help you find out the truth about that boy Hal."

I couldn't believe my ears.

"What brought this on?" I asked happily.

"It's just that you're in an impossible, no win situation here, and that's exactly the position that I was in yesterday. You got *me* out of mine, and now I want to get *you* out of yours. But first, tell me what happened after

I left the café."

"Well, I hardly dare tell you, but things are even worse with Jan. It was all right at first. She didn't mind my taking over from you and she even believed my story about you throwing up in the loo. We had a conversation through the door."

"You actually pretended to be *me*! What an actress!"

"It wasn't difficult because I muffled my voice with my jumper, and spoke very faintly as though I was heaving and retching."

Andy giggled. "You're mad, Luce. Fancy being able to do that on the spur of the moment! So, what went wrong?"

I told Andy the whole story about my confrontation with Hal at his school and then his little announcement in the café. She kept gasping and saying, "Oh, no! Oh, *no*!" And when I got to the end she said, "It's a terrible mess, but somehow we'll crack it." She decided to call a conference for all six of us at morning break, but we couldn't find Tash, Fen and Leah. Jaimini came bounding up to us though and said, "I've got something really important to tell you, Luce."

"Will it help her bring down the monster?" Andy asked, standing staunchly by me as though she wouldn't let anyone speak to me unless she was sure they were strictly on my side. Good old Andy, back to her old self. The little girl with loads of guts!

"It's about something I saw on Sunday afternoon," Jaimini explained. "I was dying to tell you yesterday, but Mum insisted I wasn't well enough to go to school and I didn't want to tell you on the phone."

"Let's go down to the netball courts," Andy suggested. So we did. On the way we met the other three and dragged them down with us. Andy carried on in her role as Detective Chief Inspector.

"Right, I want to update you all by telling you what happened yesterday, and then Jaimini's got something to report."

Everybody then listened obediently as Andy recounted the previous day's events, making me sound like a real hero in the process. It was becoming obvious to me that I was regaining my credibility and getting drawn back into the fold. I felt really happy. Jaimini then began her tale.

"On Sunday afternoon," she started, "I felt totally miserable, so Mum suggested that we all go down to the Terraced Gardens and have a walk round and a cup of tea. Well, I couldn't think of anything more boring, but I decided it would be marginally better than being depressed at home, so off we went."

The Terraced Gardens, by the way, is a really sweet sort of park just outside Cableden which attracts a lot of tourists because it's got some beautifully kept gardens with all sorts of exotic, colourful flowers and plants under a glass-covered way with fountains and little ponds amongst them. There are tiny sparkling tropical fish darting about in the ponds, and the whole place is gorgeous. I suppose we take it for granted because we've been there so often.

The rest of the Terraced Gardens is like a park. There's a bowling green at one end and a children's adventure playground, and there's also a huge lawn with a terraced area beside it — hence the name of the park. Next to the covered gardens there's a café with an indoor play area attached for children. This part is only open at the weekends.

"So we went down to the Gardens," Jaimini carried on, "and while Mum and Dad were still strolling through the covered way, I went through to the café area to have a look at those craft things they've got for sale there.

"I was just deciding whether or not to buy this lovely scented candle as a present for Mum's birthday, when I spotted Hal's mother out of the corner of my eye, so I figured Hal wouldn't be too far away. His mother seemed jittery and kept turning her head towards the play area. It was obvious she was anxious to get there and check up on Hal, but she couldn't because she was stuck in a queue at the craft stall.

"The playroom door was open so I decided to stand just outside and investigate. There were loads of children in there, while their parents were at the other end in the café bit. There were also a couple of supervisors keeping an eye on the children.

"Some very little children were playing with Lego in one corner. Others were playing with building bricks or on the racing track or in the playhouse. But it was in the far corner that I spotted Hal. I thought to myself, right, now I've got the chance to watch you. See what kind of a kid you really are. He was standing very quietly watching three other children skilfully and silently placing domino after domino after domino on their ends with so much concentration that I don't think they would have realized if the place had been on fire…"

"Oh, yes, I know," I interrupted Jaimini, "and then when you've got them all in place, you gently tap the last one, then one by one they all tip into the next one and it makes a really beautiful cascading pattern. We used to love doing that, didn't we?"

Jaimini nodded and smiled at the memory, then took up her story again.

"Anyway, what these three industrious children had set up had to be seen to be believed. They'd even got this huge bridge erected. I could see the excitement on their faces when it was all finished, and the moment they'd been looking forward to had finally arrived. Two of the children stood up and waited at the side while the third one bent down to make the magic move by tapping the lead domino. He was just about to do it when Hal suddenly deliberately kicked the dominoes and the whole lot just collapsed. I felt so absolutely furious I could have walloped that kid.

"One of the other kids did just that. He turned round and socked Hal one on the jaw, which made Hal kick him in the shin, and by that time an adult had flown over and was trying to separate them. Hal's mother rushed in and there were raised voices all round. Then out came poor Mrs Perry, holding Hal's hand tightly and looking red in the face while Hal had a defiant, unruffled air. In fact, he was practically smiling, and I had the distinct impression he had enjoyed himself in there – even when he was being told off."

"The toerag!" I said fiercely, picturing the scene perfectly and imagining those three poor children's faces as the fruits of their patient labour was destroyed with one aggressive kick.

"So you see, that's why I believe you…"

"Oh, Jaimini … you believe me… At long last *someone* believes me."

"Yes. I think that kid's capable of anything."

"It's almost like he *wants* to get into trouble."

"Attention seeking, it's called. There's usually a reason for it," Fen commented thoughtfully.

"Yes, and in Hal's case there certainly is, but I don't understand why he's got worse since Mr and Mrs Perry adopted him."

"No, that's weird, isn't it?"

"And neither do I understand why he's particularly gunning for me."

"Perhaps it's because of the twins," Tash suggested.

"But his whole fixation on me started before he knew I was the twins' sister."

"Yes, that's true."

We sat there on the netball courts, a small circle of thoughtful girls, all puzzled and frowning.

"I think we owe you a big apology," Tash finally said.

"Yes, we do," Fen added. "We're really sorry for not believing you, Luce."

"Don't worry, it's probably my fault because I usually exaggerate so much," I said happily.

"We've got to make up for it now, and help you solve your problems," Leah said.

"Yes, and we've also got to work on Jan, and get her to apologize to you," Jaimini added. That made my happiness complete because she didn't say, "We've also got to work on Jan and get her to take you back." She understood the unfairness of the way I'd been treated.

The bell for the end of break went just then, and we had to scurry back for lessons.

Before we parted though, we decided that we should all go home and try to come up with a plan of action to stop Hal from wrecking my life. Whichever plan was voted the best would be the one we'd use.

I sat in front of the TV that evening, because I often think my best thoughts in front of the TV. I don't really follow the programme I'm staring at, I just go off into my own world.

This particular evening we were all watching a documentary about the social services and the work they do. Well, the others were watching. Personally I was imagining myself all alone in a big room with Hal. I was watching him laboriously setting up a domino pattern, then just at the moment he was about to tap the last one and have the pleasure of seeing them all fall down, I grabbed him from behind, clamped his arm to his side and said, "Right, unless you tell me what your problem is, I'll kick this lot down! And there are no adults around for you to go dobbing to."

My satisfying daydream was interrupted by Terry's voice.

"She looks a bit like you, that girl…"

I glanced uninterestedly at the screen. There was a girl talking who looked about my age and did rather resemble me.

"She's the spitting image of Luce," Leo said, sitting up.

"Yeah," breathed Tim in agreement.

"Ssh," said Mum. "Listen."

The rest of the family listened but I had lost interest, except that I noticed that she was also called Lucy, which I thought was a bit of a coincidence, but then I went back to my daydream.

"I don't think she looks all that much like you, Luce," Mum said a bit later, "but it's quite a coincidence that her name is Lucy, too, *and* she's thirteen like you."

After that Terry switched the television off and the others decided to have a game of cards but I went up to my room and lay on my bed listening to music and trying to form a plan. When about thirty minutes had passed without anything wonderful springing to mind, I decided that I was wasting my time and I'd go and join the rest of the family in their card game. I just hoped that one of the other five had thought of something good.

I never made it downstairs because the phone rang and it was Tash, wondering if we could have a meeting this evening because she had practices for one thing or another in morning break and at lunchtime. I checked with Mum and Terry that it was OK, then set up the meeting at my place.

In no time at all the six of us were sitting about in my bedroom. We quickly compared notes to find that nobody had really come up with any great plan of action, but Tash pointed out that the most important thing was to try and find out more about Hal. "We need to know more about his background. There may be something very important and relevant that we're missing," she said.

"So where do we start?" I asked. "There's only Mrs Perry, and she doesn't trust me one iota, so I can't talk to her."

"I don't think she'd be very willing to talk to any of us, either. After all we're no more than strangers to her," Fen pointed out.

"What about that other woman?" Jaimini asked thoughtfully. "You said Hal was with someone else the first time you saw him, Luce."

I racked my brain. "That's right. I'd forgotten about her."

"I think you need to pump the twins for information," Leah said.

"Knowing the twins they'll want paying for the job of giving information."

"Tell them we'll buy them a milkshake and a burger each at the café if they manage to find out more about Hal."

"I think it'd be better if I just discreetly pump them, rather than make a big thing of it."

So after the girls had gone I started gently cross-examining the boys.

"Jaimini spotted that boy Hal causing havoc over the weekend," I commented conversationally to the twins as we were all helping Mum to wash up and clear up generally.

"He's always causing havoc," Tim said.

"What's havoc?" Leo asked.

"No idea, but if anyone can cause it, Eel can," Tim told his twin, with a knowing look that made me smile.

"Havoc is chaos," I explained. "Apparently Hal kicked over somebody's domino pattern that they'd spent ages setting up."

"That's nothing. He kicked Miss Watkins today," Tim told me.

"Really? What did she do?" Mum asked in a shocked tone.

"She sent him to a Place to Be."

"A Place to Be? What's that?" asked Mum.

"It's the name of this special room where you can go to talk about things," Leo explained. "Eel spends more time in there than he does in the classroom."

"Who can he talk to in there?" Mum asked.

"A special lady that comes into the school."

"Called Mrs Murray."

"She's nice. She lets you draw pictures and

play with the puppets and anything you want."

"How do you know?" Mum asked. "Have you ever been in there?"

"No, never, but Eel's told us about it."

"Yeah and shown us his pictures that he's drawn."

"What does he draw?" I asked, thinking, now we're getting somewhere.

"The same boring thing all the time."

"What's that?"

"A girl."

"What girl?"

"He says it's his sister but he's lying because he hasn't even got a sister."

My mind was ticking away.

"What does the girl look like?"

"Not like anything," Tim said scornfully.

"She's always got a scarf on," Leo added as they surreptitiously stopped helping and slipped out of the kitchen.

Mum and I turned to look at each other slowly.

"Perhaps he wishes he had a sister," Mum said softly.

We held each other's eyes as an amazing thought came into my head.

"Perhaps he imagines a sister wearing a scarf," I said carefully. "And when he saw me wearing a scarf he got angry because he realized I was someone else's sister and could never belong to him…" I paused and looked wide-eyed at Mum. "What do you think, Mum?"

"I didn't know he'd seen you in a scarf."

"Yes … he did once…" I said rather lamely, because I'd completely forgotten that Mum wasn't aware of my little outing to the café. She thought it was the corner shop I'd been to on the dreaded hair-dying day!

"I think you could be right," Mum agreed thoughtfully and without any hint of suspicion. "That doesn't mean you *are* right," she quickly added. "It means you *could* be right. So don't go jumping in with two feet, now."

But I'd gone. Not exactly jumping in with two feet, more bounding upstairs two at a time. Once in my room I got straight on the phone to Jaimini. "I think I've got something," I told her, excitedly. Then I recounted the conversation with the twins and what Mum and I had thought afterwards.

"I think you *have* got something!" Jaimini agreed equally excitedly. "What did you say was the name of the woman in the Place to Be?"

"Mrs Murray."

"She's probably the lady you saw Hal with in the first place."

"Good thinking, Jaimini. But what do you think we ought to do next?"

"I think we need to send in Andy the spy. You know what she's like – fast and subtle."

"She certainly is," I agreed, and with that we rang off, both feeling optimistic and dying to talk to Andy the next day. I would have phoned her there and then, but we wanted all to be together to discuss the next step.

It was lunchtime the following day before we got to see Andy, and she was in no mood to discuss any interesting spy work that we may have got lined up for her. She was looking pale and anxious again. I would have laid money on it being something to do with her dad, and I was right, because nothing and no one else is capable of knocking her toughness aside.

"What's up, Andy?" I asked, sitting down next to her in the canteen.

"Dad," she answered simply, staring at her food but not touching it, while the rest of us tucked in.

"What's he done now?" Jaimini asked.

Leah was sitting beside Andy. "He's suggested a little visit to the café," she explained.

"He's suspicious. I can tell," Andy said despondently. "He asked me which of my friends was working at the café today after school. I said I thought it was Tash, and he said, 'I've never met Tash. Why don't we go along and have a bite to eat after school?' Mum's taking Sebastien to Jungle Tumble so it'll just be me and Dad…" She paused, then blurted out, "I'm dreading it, Luce. I'm certain he's going to try and catch me out by talking to Jan."

We all gasped when she said that because that was the one thing no one had thought of.

"We'll have to explain all about it to Jan and get her to promise not to say anything to him," Leah said.

"No, no," Fen insisted. "Jan is not a happy lady at the moment and we mustn't risk antagonizing her. It'd only take a small thing like that to make her flip and dismiss the lot of us. No, we need to make sure we're all in the café and we'll just steer Jan, and the conversation, in the other direction all the time. It'll be hard work but we've coped with tougher problems."

As we split up for afternoon lessons, Jaimini whispered to me, "Let's just get today over with, then we'll tackle Andy about Hal. She can't concentrate on anything while her dad's on the war path."

So that day after school we all went home very briefly and told our mums that we were doing a joint project for school and that we were meeting at the café to discuss it. Andy didn't have to invent any projects, of course. She just had to turn up with her dad and introduce him to Tash, who was the first one to arrive at the café ready for work.

We'd instructed Andy to make sure she led her dad to one of the tables that Mark usually served, and Mark himself would by then have been heavily briefed to keep quiet, by Tash. We, on the other hand, all sat at one of *Jan's* tables to reduce the chance of Jan serving Andy and her dad, because the tables were only allocated to definite servers if the café was really crowded. Jan duly served us with our Cokes and lemonades and was extremely tight-lipped and cold towards us all.

Tash came out of the kitchen a minute later, watered the plants on the window-sill and whispered to us, "Jan's in a very 'iffy' mood. We mustn't let anything go wrong or she'll get rid of the lot of us… I'd better go back or she'll accuse me of wasting time."

As Tash scurried back to the kitchen, the café door opened and in came Andy and her dad. Andy made a dive for table four but her dad wasn't in so much of a hurry. He took his time looking round the café, and of course his eyes rested on us.

"Hello, Mr Sorrell," said Fen.

"Aha, your partners in crime, Agnès."

We all gulped and probably looked terribly guilty, but tried to make a show of laughing at his wit.

"Only joking," he smiled. But the smile didn't seem to reach his eyes. There was something about this man that didn't quite fit. He intrigued me. It came as quite a shock to me, but at that moment in time I realized that I didn't feel the same as the others did about Mr Superior Sorrell. In fact I wasn't scared of him at all.

"I like your tie," I said brazenly. It was only the stifled gasps of the others that made me think that my opening remark had perhaps been a touch too bold. His eyes locked into mine and there was a long pause. I held his gaze and smiled at him. I felt determined to break him. Compared to Hal, he didn't seem a problem in my life.

"Thank you," he replied, then turning rather abruptly he sat down at the table next to ours so Andy reluctantly had to follow suit. This was usually a "Jan" table, if the café was full.

Tash came out of the kitchen, saw Andy and her dad, did a quick check that no one was watching, then headed towards them. Behind her the kitchen door opened and unbeknown to Tash, Jan came in. Fen pretended to choke on her lemonade, which instantly made Tash realize that this was a warning for her, so she veered off to the left and went back into the kitchen.

"Good afternoon," Jan said politely to Mr Sorrell. "Hello, Andy. What can I get you both?"

Mr Sorrell looked at Andy with slightly raised eyebrows as if to say, "Well, aren't you going to introduce me?"

"Oh, this is Jan, Fen's aunt. This is my dad."

We all held our breath and prayed that Jan wouldn't say anything about the fact that Andy worked at the café, but all she said was,

"Very pleased to meet you, Mr Sorrell."

Andy quickly ordered Coke, and her father said that he'd have a glass of white wine if that could be arranged.

"Certainly," said Jan. "We generally only serve white wine with meals, but on this occasion…"

"That's very kind," said Mr Sorrell, with a charming smile. He then tried to persuade Andy to eat something. The poor girl probably felt sick, but nevertheless she bravely ordered a cheeseburger and we all heaved a sigh of relief as Jan disappeared.

Tash must have asked if she could take the order to Andy's table, because out she came a couple of minutes later with a Coke and a cheeseburger.

"Aha, this must be Natasha," said Mr Sorrell as she placed the order on the table and blushed a bit. She looks very pretty when she blushes, Tash does.

"Tash," she said with a smile.

"You girls and your nicknames. What is it they call you, Agnès?"

"Andy."

"Yes, then there's Fen and…"

"We don't shorten Leah's name much."

"You call me Jaimes sometimes," Jaimini offered.

"Another boy's name. And what about Lucy Edmunson?"

"We generally say Luce," Fen told him.

He smiled but it was difficult to know what he was thinking. "So you all work here, do you?"

Uh-oh! This was the six million dollar question we'd all been dreading. And somebody had to think of something quickly because Jan had appeared with Mr Sorrell's glass of white wine.

"Y…yes," we all said. OK so far because Jan couldn't tell that Andy hadn't answered…

"You must feel left out, Agnès? The only one with no work?"

At that point Fen did a spectacular swipe of her lemonade and managed to tip it partly over the table and partly over me, before I grabbed it and righted it.

"Oh, clumsy me!" she said jumping up. "I'll go and get a cloth."

Jan had that long suffering "not-again" look on her face, and her eyes were on me. Instantly, we all realized what she was thinking. She'd only noticed me catching the lemonade, and assumed that Fen was covering up for my clumsiness.

Fen returned with the cloth but Jan snatched it from her and started vigorously wiping up the spilt lemonade without looking at any of us.

"Jan, it was *my* mistake. *I* spilt it," Fen ventured.

"Luce only caught it. She saved it from breaking," Jaimini tried.

Still Jan made no comment. She just turned on her heel and went back into the kitchen. Tash hadn't moved from Andy's table throughout this. Mr Sorrell decided to strike up a conversation with her. "And what exactly are your duties here?"

"Um … well, you have to be here at four o'clock…"

"At four?"

"Yes. And you just basically wash up and help Jan in any way you can. We don't often take orders or serve food, but I asked if I could this time."

"Mm, I see," Mr Sorrell said, but it was obvious he wasn't really listening. His eyes had moved away from Tash and he was looking at something big and bright which was hanging up on the hat stand. I clapped my hand to my mouth as I realized that it was Terry's golf umbrella that I had left there the other day.

"Lucy – I mean Luce, I'm sorry," said Mr Sorrell with that sarcastic edge to his voice, "you left your umbrella behind… It *is* yours, isn't it?"

I gulped and wondered briefly how much mileage there would be in claiming no knowledge of the umbrella, but he was looking at me in such a way that I knew he knew it was mine.

I nodded and tried for a light, unconcerned tone as I said, "Yes, that's mine, I must have left it when I came to work the other day."

He smiled at me, then turned back to Tash. "So you start work at four o'clock, you say?"

"Yes," said Tash innocently.

Andy and I exchanged uneasy glances. We both knew exactly how his mind was working. Mr Sorrell looked first at me, then at Andy. His eyes glinted ominously. He knew that that was me hiding under the umbrella and he knew that I couldn't have got to the café before half past four that day. So why had I been half an hour late for work?

Over the rim of his glass his eyes rested on Andy while she seemed to wither visibly in her seat.

Chapter 7

Eventually the atmosphere became un-bearable. Tash slipped back into the kitchen and we all turned away from Mr Sorrell and Andy, into our own whispered conversation.

At first we kept to safe topics – homework and the like – but as we gradually realized that at the next table Mr Sorrell and Andy were actually talking, and didn't appear to be taking much notice of us, I told the girls about the golfing umbrella and how I felt sure that Mr Sorrell's interrogation and the hard look he had then given Andy, all pointed to the fact that he had guessed the truth. He now knew

Andy had defied him and that she was working at the café.

"He makes me sick," I whispered to Jaimini, Leah and Fen. How dare he be such a dictator! "And Jan makes me sick too," I added with feeling. "She blames me for absolutely everything that goes wrong. I bet if the electricity suddenly went off in here, she'd say, 'Lucy, it was obviously you. You were only twenty metres from the main fuse box. It *had* to be you…'"

Fen and the others giggled, but I was getting more and more wound up. "I'm surprised she doesn't blame me for all the world's natural disasters… I mean, that flood in Holland, let's face it, I must have had *something* to do with it…"

Leah laughed out loud at that, and I noticed Andy get up to go to the loo. At least that was her excuse. I bet she really wanted to get away from that hateful father of hers. "Just look at him," I hissed vehemently at the other three, "sitting there like King Claptrap… I'm going to pull him down a peg or two."

I stood up, and immediately the expression on my three friends' faces turned to alarm. "No," said Jaimini, trying to drag me back down again. "You mustn't!"

It was too late. I had the bit well and truly between my teeth. Andy was still in the loo. I took her place and faced Mr Sorrell with a fierce look on my face.

"OK, Mr Sorrell," I said, in what I realized afterwards must have been quite a loud voice, "I know you know what's going on here. Yes, you're right, that *is* my umbrella. And that *was* me you saw going to work the other day. And yes, I *was* late because it wasn't really my turn. It was Andy's, but of course she couldn't do it because of you!"

I was aware of the gasps and then tension all around me. "Your own daughter is actually frightened of you, Mr Sorrell … and do you know what we call her? We call her the daring one. So that must make you some kind of *ogre*!"

I stopped there, partly because Andy was standing beside me but mainly because someone had clamped a hand on my shoulder, and it was not one of my friends. I looked up to see Jan looking absolutely furious. Quite honestly I don't think I would have been surprised if she'd handcuffed me at that moment.

"Lucy, *will* you be quiet!" she practically spat at me. "You are causing a scene as usual. I don't know what nonsense you're telling Mr Sorrell, but I've had enough of you – lying about that boy, lying about Andy being ill, lying about that drink you just spilt, and no doubt lying to Mr Sorrell, as well…"

"Er, excuse me, if I could just throw a little light on it all," Mr Sorrell said with a nice boyish smile for Jan, which made her words fade away and a big blush come creeping up from her neck. "I would say that Lucy is certainly impulsive, but not a liar… No, certainly not a liar. I can't comment on the first two things you mentioned, but she certainly didn't spill the drink. It was Fenella who did that. I saw it quite clearly. And she certainly hasn't told me any lies. Quite the reverse, actually. In fact, she's the only one of these girls who's brave enough to confront me with the truth, which incidentally, I've been suspicious about for some time."

As Mr Sorrell had been speaking, a very peculiar thing had happened to me. I felt like a balloon with all the air going out of it, but in this case it was the anger going out of me. Andy's face was white, I noticed; Jan's was red, and the rest of the girls, including Tash who had joined us at some point, were looking very nervous, eyes darting everywhere.

Mr Sorrell suddenly leaned forward and gave Jan's hand a friendly pat, which made her blush even more. "Thank you for your concern. I wonder, could I have another glass of white wine, and also more drinks for these girls?"

He smiled and sat back in his chair as though he'd just made a very satisfactory business deal. I stood up and started to go back to my place, but Mr Sorrell's next words stopped me in my tracks.

"If Agnès is the daring one, what on earth

do they call you, Lucy? The totally crazy one?"

We all cracked up laughing at that. "Yes, we do!" Fen spluttered. Andy herself just smiled, then she and her dad carried on talking. I noticed their conversation became more and more intense.

Meanwhile on our table the other three congratulated me out of the sides of their mouths, and rolled their eyes and giggled. We chatted and laughed, and occasionally whispered and wondered what was going on between Andy and her dad.

In a strange sort of way I felt quite proud of myself, but also quite worried. I wasn't sure if I'd made things worse or better. I kept trying to catch Andy's eye but she was deep in conversation with her dad. I was dying to find out the next day what he'd been saying to her. His reaction in front of us was brilliant compared with how I'd thought it was going to be, but I couldn't help worrying in case he was saving up for a big explosion as soon as he got Andy away from the café. I'd never forgive myself if that happened, because I would be directly responsible.

I walked home thoughtfully when we'd all parted ways. Mr Sorrell had handed me the umbrella and said, "Don't forget about this. You might need it just in case you want to hide from someone." I had gone pink but grinned at that, and he had grinned back which had given another boost to my courage.

"You're not going to be cross with Andy later?" I had asked him tentatively.

"I'll try not to be," he had replied, looking serious, but I was sure I saw the corner of his mouth twitch.

As I walked home I thought to myself, the old geezer's definitely softening up. Or maybe we misjudged him. Maybe it does him good to be stood up to occasionally? I was so deep in thought about Mr Sorrell that I didn't see Hal until I was practically on top of him. He was just standing there, barring my way.

Instinctively I looked round to see if his mother was there, or any other adult, then when I realized he was quite alone I decided to try to put him at his ease because there was nothing to be gained from going in heavy. I'd already made that mistake.

I put my hands up and said, "Don't shoot, I surrender," with a big grin. He didn't react at all to that. No laugh, no smile, no cross retort. Just an impassive expression and silence.

I began to feel uneasy. "OK, what's this all about?" I said, my eyes narrowing suspiciously. "What amazing stunt are you going to pull this time to get me into trouble? Hmm?"

Still he just eyed me silently. "If you're not even going to speak to me, I may as well carry on home," I told him firmly. But I hesitated because half of me was afraid of walking past him in case he'd set up some weird and wonderful trap for me. I wouldn't have put anything past him, the way his mind worked.

"Nobody believes me," he suddenly said. His words hung in the air, and I waited, wondering what was to follow. "Do you know what that feels like?" he asked me softly.

"Yes, yes, I do," I replied. It was of course because of Hal himself that I knew only too well what that felt like.

"You see, you look like her," he stated, flatly. I was trying as hard as I could to piece together his little bits of information. I didn't want to say the wrong thing to make him stop talking, but on the other hand I wasn't sure what was the right thing to say.

"Who do I look like?" I asked gently.

"Who do you think?" he snapped. "Your brothers must have told you."

"They … they told me about the Place to Be," I tried carefully.

"You look like that!" he said, thrusting a picture under my nose, as though I hadn't spoken at all. I'd hardly glanced at the picture when he pulled it away. I'd seen enough though. It was a picture he'd drawn himself of a girl with a blue skirt and a coloured scarf.

"Who is it?" I asked.

"You won't believe me. Nobody does."

"Is it … your sister?" I ventured.

He jerked his face upwards to mine. His eyes were challenging me to look as though I didn't believe him, and I realized in that instant that he needed someone to believe him as desperately as I had needed someone to believe me a few days before.

"Let me see the picture again," I asked, and very cautiously he held out his childish picture to me.

"I *know* I've got a sister," he said, "even though nobody will talk about her."

"And she looks like me?"

He nodded.

"Tell me how you know," I said.

"I just know. I've always known. She's somewhere... And anyway, I've seen a photo of her... Lucy, she's called... Same as you."

"Did you think I *was* your sister?"

Again he nodded. "I really thought I'd found her at last, because when you had that scarf on, you looked like the photo."

"What photo? Where did you see a photo of her?"

"Before I had any foster parents, I had lots

of social workers, and one of them had the photo on one of her papers all about me. They don't want me to find her... It's even worse now because I haven't got any social workers, 'cause I'm properly adopted, see. That means I'll never find my sister, specially when she's in another country very far away..."

So this explained why Hal's behaviour had apparently got worse since his adoption.

"Why do you think that?" I asked, trying to keep my voice level so he wouldn't see how upset I felt for him. I was getting a horrible sinking feeling. I knew that social workers always went out of their way to keep brothers and sisters together, so if they didn't want Hal to know about his sister, something must have happened to her ... if there was a sister in the first place.

"I just do," he said with a hopeless shrug. It was all very confusing. Was it that nobody believed him? Or was it that nobody wanted to talk about it because his sister had disappeared, or worst of all, had died? Either way, the outlook looked bleak for the desperate little boy beside me. "You will help me, won't you?" he was saying.

I didn't hesitate. I knew how hesitation made you feel. "Yes, I will. Course I will."

He smiled. For the first time ever he gave me a genuine smile. "Where shall we start looking?" he asked, eyes shining with confidence.

"First we need to plan a campaign," I told him, trying to sound positive. "We mustn't rush in. I know, *you* go home, and I'll do some good hard thinking, and we'll meet here tomorrow after school."

"OK," he said with innocent trust. He was looking at my hand. His own hand was raised. I realized what he was waiting for. I raised my hand and he slapped my palm hard. "*Yo!*" he declared. "See ya!"

And off he ran, weaving haphazardly all over the pavement and singing loudly as he went. I stood and watched him until he was out of sight – a little spidery boy scuttling off to nowhere in particular. I felt stuck to the ground. My brain was doing somersaults. And with every somersault were the words "What now?" "What now?" I'd given him hope. I must have been crazy. There may not *be* any hope. Why oh why was I so impulsive? I had really lived up to my nickname this time.

Dragging my feet, I eventually got home and once inside the kitchen, flopped into a chair, put my arms on the table and rested my head on my arms.

"Looks like a serious case of I-have-had-enough. What do you think, Melanie?" Terry joked with Mum, as they regarded me, heads on one side, arms folded.

"Help me with these chicken casseroles and tell me all about it, love," Mum said, as she turned back to her cooking. It must have been quite a big catering order because she had every ring of both our cookers on the go, and I could see that the ovens were full.

So Terry, Mum and I worked together on the chicken casseroles and I told them all about the conversation I'd just had with Hal.

At first Mum and Terry were very negative and dubious about the whole thing.

"You mustn't give him hope if there isn't any," Mum pointed out gravely.

"It's obviously very big in his mind," Terry commented thoughtfully.

I heard a scuffling noise just outside the kitchen door. I opened it quickly and there stood the twins. Leo practically fell into the kitchen with Tim just behind him. They'd obviously had their ears to the door.

"Go away, you big earwigs," I told them straight.

"She called us earwigs! Tell 'er off!" Leo demanded of Mum.

"Who's she? The cat's mother?" Mum asked automatically.

"No the big pig's mother," Tim said, grinning widely at something which was so pathetically unfunny.

"We're having a private conversation in here, so buzz off," Terry said.

"We know. We heard!" they chanted. "And it's not very interesting," Leo added.

"Good. Well forget it, then," Mum said. "And now go and do something constructive for a change."

They went without any fuss, but that must have been because there was about to be something good on TV. As the door closed behind them Terry frowned deep in thought.

"A penny for them," Mum said, only just missing him as she transferred a frying pan of chicken pieces into a casserole.

"I was just thinking about that programme last night... You know, the social services programme with that girl in it ... the one who looked like Luce."

Mum stopped what she was doing and gave Terry her full attention.

"Same name, same age, same scarf..."

"Don't get carried away. It's a long shot," Mum said, keeping her feet firmly on the floor.

"But worth a try," Terry persisted.

Then they were both frowning.

"I'll make a few phone calls," Terry said noncommittally.

"But why was that girl on TV?" I asked, not really understanding where this conversation was getting us because I hadn't actually been concentrating on the programme at the time.

"It was a documentary about kids in care," Terry explained. "She was one of them. Apparently she ran away from another country to try and get away from her parents, and they've tried to trace the parents but without any luck. The girl is saying she doesn't want to go back to them, anyway," Terry explained.

My eyes widened and I suddenly felt very lucky. "Thanks Terry," I said, giving him an impulsive kiss.

"Now, whatever you do, *don't* say anything to Hal," Mum instructed me, seriously. "Just tell him you're working on his case. Make it sound as important as possible without actually saying anything concrete. Meanwhile I'll pop down to the school and see if I can catch that Mrs Murray, the lady in the Place to Be."

The next day the six of us belted down to the netball courts in morning break, at record speed so we'd have the longest possible time to hear what Andy had to say. Nobody knew that I had a tale to tell as well, but I wanted to check that Andy was all right first.

She wasn't looking herself. She seemed listless and depressed and we feared the worst. "So what did he say afterwards?" I asked straight away. "Please, *please* tell me I didn't ruin everything with my big mouth."

"No, you didn't ruin anything, don't worry," Andy said rather flatly. "Dad thinks you're the greatest thing since sliced bread actually…"

"What? Me?" I couldn't believe my ears because people often admire Andy as she's so daring and so sporty, like a little power pack; they often admire Jaimini because of her brains and her beauty; they often admire Fen because of her single-mindedness; they admire Leah because of her great musical talent; they admire Tash because she's wise and sensible, but nobody has ever admired me because I'm just an impulsive girl with a big mouth.

"You cannot be serious," I said in a strong American accent, which made the others laugh, all except Andy, who obviously was serious – very.

"Well," she began with a big sigh, "he's cross about the café. Says I shouldn't have gone behind his back and all that, but apart from that it's almost as though the café is a little side issue because he said he'd already guessed ages ago that I was working there.

"Strangely enough, though, he seems to be attaching more importance to the fact that I didn't have the guts to tell him. That's why he thinks you're so great Luce, because you stood up to him. He can't believe that I'm supposed to be the daring one. He kept on and on about that. He wanted to know how I got that tag in the first place. And when I tried to think, I couldn't come up with a single reason why. I felt so stupid and pathetic. I'm sure he thinks I'm useless."

Leah put her arm round Andy and said that nobody could possibly think she was useless. Then we all tried to cheer Andy up, but nothing did any good even when Tash very sensibly said, "Well, at least you can work in the café without having to worry from now on, can't you?"

"I suppose so. He seems to have accepted it for the moment. But you can never tell with Dad. He could suddenly veto the whole thing for no apparent reason, but certainly at the moment it seems all right, so thanks very much, Luce."

I smiled. We should have been jubilant but we weren't, and nobody was quite sure why.

"This is ridiculous," Leah said, voicing all our thoughts. "We ought to be celebrating, and instead we're sitting here morose as ducks in a desert!"

"It's my fault," Andy admitted with a sigh. "I just feel that I'm such a disappointment to him. I even heard him telling Mum about Luce's outburst, and he was actually laughing about it. 'She certainly has got guts, that

Lucy girl,' I heard him say as he shook his head in amazement as though you'd just sailed single-handed round the world in a chocolate wrapper or something."

We had to laugh, despite Andy's miserable face. "Perhaps I ought to be renamed the *witty* one," she said cynically.

"Don't be silly," we disagreed whole-heartedly. "You're the daring one, always were and always will be!"

"Not in Dad's eyes, I'm not … not till I prove it."

After that I told them all about Hal and the conversation I'd had with Mum and Terry afterwards. My story caused great interest and excitement.

"I saw that programme too!" Fen said. "And Terry's right. That girl *did* look like you. Do you think she could be Hal's long-lost sister?"

"I don't know. Mum and Terry seemed very doubtful…"

"I don't see how he could have got separated from his sister in the first place…" Jaimini said thoughtfully.

"Perhaps he started off by imagining a sister, and after a bit he even began to believe in it himself," suggested Leah.

"If he was only two when his parents left him, he wouldn't have been old enough to know what was going on, would he?" Fen pointed out.

"Hmm, I don't know," Tash said with a frown.

"Me neither," Andy added. They were obviously both thinking about their own little brother and sister.

"Let us know if anything happens, won't you?" Fen said.

"I'll phone if there's anything amazing to report. Otherwise I'll see you tomorrow."

"Don't phone me before six-thirty," Andy said, "because I'll be working at the café. Oh and by the way, how was Jan yesterday after everything had died down?" she asked Tash.

Tash wrinkled her nose for answer. I began to wonder if Jan would ever get back to normal again. She used to be so easy going, so firm yet so fair, and now she seemed to be in a permanent bad mood.

"It's all my fault," I said with a huge sigh, but Fen wasn't so sure.

"I was talking about Jan to Mum the other day, and Mum said Jan was going through a difficult time at the moment and that we all had to try and be a bit more tolerant and understanding than usual."

"Oh dear," I said, beginning to feel guilty again.

"What do you think your mum meant?" Tash asked.

"Your guess is as good as mine. I'm just telling you what she said."

When the end of break bell rang a few minutes later it was six puzzled girls who came back from the netball courts and parted ways for the next lesson. We suddenly seemed to be surrounded by puzzles – Jan … Hal … Andy's dad…

Chapter 8

I waited for Hal for twenty minutes at the same place where we had met the previous day, before deciding he wasn't going to turn up. I was more than perplexed by this. I was bewildered because I had thought this whole thing about finding his sister was the most important thing in his life.

As I walked slowly home I started to imagine what might have happened. Perhaps now that he'd actually talked about the possibility of finding his sister, he had come to terms with reality. Maybe he realized now that it had all been his imagination. Yes, after all it was an excellent way of getting lots of attention, but he'd become scared when someone like me actively started to follow up his story. Poor Hal.

The kitchen windows were coated with steam and there was a lovely pungent atmosphere in there, as I went in to say "Hi" to Mum. The twins were walking around like a couple of inspectors, sticking their noses into this pan and that casserole, occasionally dipping their fingers in and sampling the dishes.

"Wash those fingers!" Mum instructed them, as she always did, but they'd developed the habit of keeping the tap running and sticking their fingers under it then giving them a quick dry on the towel between each dip.

"I've been run off my feet," was Mum's greeting to me, as she dashed about with a pair of oven gloves, putting hot dishes on a table full of other hot dishes.

"So you didn't get to see Mrs Murray?" I asked.

"'Fraid not," Mum replied. "I'll be less hassled tomorrow though."

"That's OK. It's not really worth it, anyway," I said despondently.

"What do you mean, not worth it?" she asked.

"Well, Hal didn't turn up. I couldn't believe it. I waited for ages."

"Eel's run away," Tim said in a matter-of-fact voice, as though he was letting us know his sweatshirt needed washing.

"What do you mean, run away?" I asked, feeling a rising panic. Even Mum stopped her whirlwind activities and let her oven glove drop on to the floor.

"He's just run away," Leo added, which was incredibly helpful.

"Where's he gone?" I shouted impatiently, grabbing Tim by the shoulders and forcing him round to face me.

"I've told you, he's run away! You don't tell people where you're going when you run away, do you?"

"But where *might* he have gone?" I demanded, feeling my spirits plummeting.

Leo and Tim looked at me pityingly, as

though they sympathized with me for having such poor mental capabilities, but there was really nothing they could do about it.

"If you don't know where, do you know *why*?" Mum asked, trying for a calm approach. "Have you any idea at all? Has your teacher any idea?"

"No. She was asking us lot that question, but how should we know? We can't mind-read, can we?"

"*You* didn't say anything to him, did you?" Mum asked them suspiciously.

"I said, 'Give us a bite of your Twix, Eel,' but I don't think that made him run away," Tim told us gravely.

"I said that you lot were all talking about him yesterday," Leo added, peering into one of the ovens.

Mum and I swooped on him when he said that. "Yes? What else did you say?" Mum wanted to know.

"I only said the truth," Leo answered, protestingly.

"What sort of truth?" I demanded.

"I told him what I heard Mum say, that's all."

"What *did* you hear Mum say?" I asked, trying not to lose patience.

"She said, 'You mustn't give him hope because there isn't any.'"

"Oh, no!" I squealed. "You told Hal that?"

"Well … yes," Leo stammered, suddenly realizing that perhaps he might have said the wrong thing, but not really understanding what the big deal was. "And then I told him what Terry said," he went on, "only because he wanted to know…" Leo turned a bit red.

"Yes," I snapped at him. "And what little gem of Terry's did you pass on? Hmm?"

"I only said that Terry said it was all in his mind," Leo mumbled looking anxious, as Mum and I exchanged wide-eyed that's-blown-it looks.

"Terry didn't say that at all, Leo. He said that it was really *big* in Hal's mind," I corrected my brother in an exasperated tone.

"Never mind, love," Mum said generously. "You obviously didn't realize."

Leo was almost in tears by this time. "Is it my fault that Eel's run away?" he asked, weakly.

"No, no. You're not to blame at all," Mum reassured him, "but I'd better phone his mother, I think."

Mum spent ages on the phone with Mrs Perry, going over and over what Leo had said to Hal. She kept having to explain things and go back to old conversations. Throughout this I sat with my elbows on the kitchen table and my knuckles pressed hard into my cheeks.

When finally she put the phone down, Mum said, "Poor Mrs Perry is frantic with worry. The police have taken a description and loads of details, but Mrs Perry can't help them at all with where Hal may possibly have gone."

"What about the café?" I suddenly said, jumping up. "Let me phone Andy – see if he's been in there."

"Hi, Becky," I said a moment later. "It's Luce. Can you get me Andy, please? It's quite important."

"Two seconds," said Becky, which was a phrase I'd often heard used in the café. Andy came on the phone almost immediately.

"What's happened?" she asked in a worried voice.

"I'm phoning because apparently Hal's run away, and I just wondered whether or not he'd been in the café."

"Well yes, funnily enough he did come in."

"He *did*!" I screeched down the phone. "Is he still there or what?"

"No, he's gone. Becky told me actually. She said he came in at about two-thirty. He stood by the counter looking very lost, and Becky asked him where his mum was. He didn't answer, he just handed her an envelope which said MANAGER on it. He asked if Becky would give it to the lady in charge; said it was important…"

"So the letter was for Jan?" I asked, feeling more mystified by the minute.

"Yes, Becky said the spelling was really sweet. He'd spelt 'manager', MANIDJER."

"But what did it say? Why did he write a

note to Jan of all people? Can you go and ask Jan if there were any clues in it at all?"

So Andy went off to find Jan, and it was Jan herself who came on the phone a moment later. She sounded very odd. Her voice was rather wavery. "It wasn't a long letter, Lucy… It was … well… I'll tell you another time. The only thing that's important at the moment is what he wrote at the very beginning of the letter. He said he was going away to a place that would get him his sister back. I didn't even read the letter straight away," Jan went on. "First Becky forgot to give it me, then when she did give it me, I was busy serving, and I stuffed it in my apron pocket and didn't think any more about it for about half an hour. When I read it I was so worried, I got on the phone to the school straight away."

"OK. Thanks Jan … I'll see you…"

"Yes … see you."

It was an awkward end to the conversation but I didn't have time to think about it at that moment. I wanted to rack my brain as to where Hal might have gone.

"What time of day did you talk to Hal, Leo?" Mum asked, after I'd filled her in on what Jan had said.

"It was in the dinner queue," answered a very subdued Leo.

Think Lucy, think! I told myself urgently. Go right back to the very first time you ever set eyes on the kid and think of anything you've ever heard him say.

My mind went into overdrive as I tried to recall every moment I had ever spent in Hal's company. For some reason I kept coming back to the party. It can't have been the best birthday party in the world for that poor little Ben Bridge… Ben… Yes, that was it!

"I've got it!" I cried out to Mum. "Give me the phone, I must talk to Mrs Perry."

Five minutes later Mum and I were belting off in the car to pick up Mrs Perry, having left Tim and Leo with old Mrs Sands from next door, who said she'd make them pancakes with chocolate topping, to the twins' delight.

"How can you be so sure Hal'll be there?" Mrs Perry asked me.

"I can't be a hundred per cent sure, but it's a hunch I've got."

Mrs Perry was biting her thumbnail as Mum drove along tapping the steering wheel. I was leaning forward in the back seat with the seat-belt cutting into my shoulder, but I was too tense to lean back. Mrs Perry was bombarding me with questions like, why was Hal obsessed with me? And what had I been doing at his school the other day? I answered everything as best I could, and finally told her about the drawings he'd shown me.

"He insists that he's got a sister," I said carefully to Mrs Perry.

I thought she hadn't heard me at first because she took so long to answer.

"He *has*," she finally said.

"He *has*?" My voice came out as a squeak.

"Yes," she replied wearily. "Let me start at the beginning. His parents left him when he was two. No one really understands why. His mum took him to a busy shopping centre one day and told him to wait on a certain corner until she got back. He was still waiting there five hours later."

I felt tears come into my eyes. "Where did this happen?" I asked.

"In a town called Lyrington, which is miles away from here and also several miles away from where they lived. It took quite a while to sort out who the little boy was, and by the time the authorities had got to the bottom of it, Hal's parents must have left the country. They were traced to Canada by the International Social Workers Organization, but they made it quite clear they no longer wanted him.

"Rumour had it that the father had an instant aversion to the child from the moment he was born. It's quite possible that Hal's mother feared for his safety. Perhaps the father had threatened to harm Hal or something. It sounds cruel to leave him like she did, but nobody can tell whether or not she was actually being cruel to be kind.

"Almost immediately, Hal went into a foster

home. Unfortunately, though, he was always difficult and disruptive. He started talking about his sister even at this time. It turned out that there *had* been a sister that the parents had taken away with them. She must have been seven or eight at the time when Hal was abandoned. There was no attempt made to take her away from her parents because she was in her rightful place and they were looking after her perfectly well.

"Of course, everybody thought it kinder not to mention her to Hal, and hope that in time his memory of her would fade. It seemed incredible that he'd grimly held on to the memory for as long as he had, especially when you consider that he'd been such a tiny little boy when he'd last seen her.

"He changed to another foster mother and father when he was five. That was very short-lived. They already had two children of their own, and I gather that Hal was so difficult that they gave in, in the end. So he went to a home."

Mrs Perry interrupted herself. "We seem to

be going an awfully long way. He can't have walked this far…"

She was right. Even though he'd had quite a head start, I wasn't sure that he could have done it on foot, and we weren't even there yet. "He must have got a lift or something…" My words trailed away. "Carry on about Hal," I then said, to try to keep Mrs Perry on a positive track.

"Not long after he'd gone to the home, my husband and I appeared on the scene. We hadn't got any children of our own and had been wanting children desperately for some years. We were so determined to make it work with Hal. We needed him as much as he needed us, you see. Poor little soul. But even despite that, there were times when I could have wept because I felt such a failure when everybody complained about his behaviour wherever we went.

"As time went on I found myself defending him more and more, and of course that made people very wary of me. I was becoming isolated. The fact that I was continually sticking up for Hal, even though I knew in my heart that he was to blame, made people start avoiding me. I did so want little Ben's birthday party to be a success, because Mrs Bridge was one of the very few people I knew who was prepared to tolerate Hal."

Here Mrs Perry stopped talking and I saw her rub her hand across her face. I guessed she was wiping a tear away and I felt really sorry for her.

"Did he talk about his sister to you?" I asked her.

"Oh yes, all the time, but you can imagine my dilemma. I could hardly say, 'Well, you'll never see her again so you may as well forget all about her.' And neither did I want to lie to him by saying, 'You're just imagining her. You haven't even *got* a sister.' So I've always just tried to change the subject somehow.

"He thought I didn't believe him, and I found it was easiest to keep it that way, because I didn't have to lie directly, but on the other hand, neither did I have to tell the horrible, hurtful truth. You see, in some strange way, the possibility that he *may* one day see his sister again, stopped him from being totally screwed up. I can't tell you the number of times I wished I could have waved a magic wand and brought his sister back to him."

Again Mrs Perry wiped a tear from her face. Mum's fingers had stopped drumming on the steering wheel and she was casting many sympathetic glances at Mrs Perry while driving along.

"Then Mrs Murray came into his life, and it seemed to me that she was coping with Hal much better than I could, and that upset me too."

"What about me? Did *I* upset you?" I asked quietly.

"You worried me. You see, Hal seemed so disturbed after he'd met you. It was as though you had come along and got him all stirred up, just when I thought he was beginning to settle down.

"I didn't make the connection, you see. It never dawned on me that he'd got you down for his sister. I suppose I was still thinking of her as an eight-year-old, not a thirteen-year-old as she would be by now. Lucy, she was called. I should have clicked on, shouldn't I? But I never did. I thought it was something to do with your twin brothers."

"Did Hal ever tell you that he'd seen a photo of his sister?"

"No!" Mrs Perry said in a shocked voice as she turned round to look at me. "No, he never said anything about that."

"Apparently he saw the photo attached to some papers that a social worker had."

"Oh my goodness, so it wasn't just a feeling that he had. It was more than that. He's actually seen the proof."

"Yes, and she was wearing a scarf in the picture. That's why he always draws pictures of her with a scarf on, and that's why something clicked when he first set eyes on me. I was wearing a scarf, you see."

Mrs Perry looked as though she could have cried a river. "I just hope and pray that I can get him back – even with all his problems."

I was on the point of mentioning the TV programme we'd seen, but there was no point in raising Mrs Perry's hopes at this very early stage, and anyway we were nearly there. I kept quiet till Mum stopped the car.

We had arrived at the Rolling Dippies. I don't know what the real name is for the Rolling Dippies. We've called it by this nickname ever since the twins were about five and we used to come for walks here. Tim and Leo thought of the name between them. It's a lovely, rambling, hilly place, and when you first approach it, you see dips and curves and rises in the land. But in the main it sinks down into the wide valley. When the wind is blowing on the long grass, it looks as though the land is actually rolling. Hence the nickname – Rolling Dippies.

In the valley there is a fast flowing river, wide and stony with a high waterfall that crashes down into it, so noisily that you can't hear yourself speak if you're standing near it. Further along the valley the land rises steeply and rockily at each side. And even further along a huge bridge with strong steel girders crosses above. The whole area is very popular with hikers and ramblers.

From the waterfall to the bridge, you have to choose your route. You either take the high path or the low path because it's so steep and dangerous in between. The bridge is wide enough for cars, and people often cross it especially to look down at the magnificent view and to decide where to walk, though most hikers prefer the rolling bit.

"Is this it?" Mrs Perry asked, looking this way and that to try and scan every inch of land around her. I was busy scouring the land, too. I must admit I had thought he would be in sight. My heart was beginning to beat more urgently.

"He can't be much further on," I said thoughtfully.

"Either we walk from here, or otherwise I'll have to drive right round the other way and make directly for the bridge," Mum said.

"Why here? Why the bridge?" Mrs Perry wanted to know.

"It's called Bengley Bridge," I explained. As I said those words I suddenly had a crystal clear memory of Hal at that birthday party in the café, as I had done earlier on. I told Mrs Perry.

"Hal kept teasing Ben, calling him Bengley Bridge and laughing his head off. Ben wasn't too happy about it and in the end Mrs Bridge told Hal to be quiet…"

"Where was I during this?" Mrs Perry asked me.

"You were taking a group of girls to the loo. Anyway, Hal turned on Mrs Bridge and said, 'You should be pleased, not cross, because Bengley Bridge is magic.' Mrs Bridge looked totally baffled and Hal said, 'Our teacher told us all about it. It's magic.'

"When I got home from the café that day I asked the twins if they knew anything about it and they said that Miss Watkins had been talking about the very old days before the bridge was even erected. Apparently it was a popular superstition that if you stood on the ridge to the side of where the bridge is now, good luck would come and find you. It seems that in the old days people used to go there from miles away in the hope of getting good luck."

"Oh," said Mrs Perry in a long drawn out sigh. "That sounds like the kind of story that would appeal to Hal. He's always been a superstitious boy with a big imagination. And come to think about it, he's always had a thing about bridges. Just recently he kicked over some children's lovely intricate pattern of dominoes just because it had a bridge in it, and he'd heard that it was bad luck to build bridges indoors." Mrs Perry's voice had begun to quaver. I thought back to what Jaimini had seen in the Terraced Gardens. So it wasn't just malevolence that had made him kick those dominoes down.

"Poor little chap. He thinks he'll get his sister back, doesn't he?" She was almost in tears. It was Mum who switched us all into action mode.

"Never mind," she said positively. "At least he'll get his mum back…"

"Not his real one."

"You're much more of a real mum than ever his natural mother was. Now come on. We've got to find him yet."

We decided it would be better to walk towards the bridge, so as not to frighten him by coming across him too suddenly, so we got out of the car and began walking.

We trudged along in silence scanning the land all around us, but especially focusing on the bridge ahead of us. The nearer we got, the clearer it was becoming that Hal wasn't there, unless he was right on the other side of the bridge.

"Looks like I may have been wrong," I said softly and despondently to Mum.

"We're not giving in yet. Come on," Mum said, striding out determinedly.

"What if he's not here at all? What if he's gone somewhere completely different?" said Mrs Perry. "Oh dear, and we're wasting all this time here…"

"What if he decides to go home?"

"Mr Perry is at home, dear," said Mrs Perry, patting my arm distractedly.

"Look! Look! I can see someone!" I cried out, indicating the tiny figure on the bridge. "I knew it!" I breathed.

"Clever girl," said Mrs Perry. "Come on, let's go and get him."

"We'll have to take the upper path from here," Mum said. She stopped and thought for a moment. "I wonder if it would be quicker to go back to the car and drive round by the road…"

"No, not now we're this near," I said. "Another hundred metres and we'll be within calling out distance." As I said that, it began to rain.

"Hal! Hal!" shouted Mrs Perry. He didn't appear to hear her at first. "At least we can see that it *is* him now," she said with relief. "Hal! Over here!"

He turned then, and looked at us. "I don't want you here," he shouted back in a voice trembling with anger and grief.

"I've come to take you home," Mrs Perry called back. We all stood still as statues, watching and listening.

"I'm not coming back," Hal shouted aggressively. "I want my sister back."

"I know you do, love," Mrs Perry called back, but I doubt that Hal would have heard her because her voice was too weak with sadness.

"We want to help you, Hal," I yelled out.

"No, you don't. Leo told me," came the impassioned voice.

"Leo got it wrong," I shouted back.

"Don't raise his hopes," Mum said, sounding a note of caution.

"I won't say anything that isn't true," I told her, "but if we don't give him some hope we'll never get him down."

Cautiously we moved closer so we wouldn't need to shout so much, but Hal, seeing us moving in on him, started to climb up the side of the bridge.

"No, Hal! You mustn't!" his mother screeched. "It's dangerous. You'll fall!" she added, almost hysterically.

"I want to fall!" Hal called back defiantly.

"No! No! Hal! Please!" Mrs Perry's voice

rang out in anguish and desperation over the Rolling Dippies where the rain was falling in slanting curtains. But up on the bridge little Hal stood dangerously high. His mother had stopped shouting and stood rooted to the spot, but we all heard her whispered plea before it floated away on the wind...

"*Please*, don't let him fall."

Chapter 9

I don't know if you've ever felt as though a moment in your life has been frozen in time, but for me, this was the second time I'd had that feeling. The first time was when Tim had been two and he had stood on a chair, opened the door that leads up to the attic, gone up the narrow stairs, put another chair in front of the window, climbed up to the broad window-sill, where you could actually sit, opened the window and stood up on the ledge waving and grinning at Mum, Terry, Leo and me, who were in the garden.

It had been a wonderful summer's day and Tim had only gone into the kitchen to get his ball which had bounced inside. Somehow he must have got side-tracked and climbed the stairs and then the attic stairs. I'll never forget the moment when our happy game of bat and ball in the garden was frozen into a scene of horror as Mum screamed, "Don't move, Tim. Don't move!"

Terry had stood below, one hand shielding his eyes from the sun as he looked up at the attic window, and kept up a desperate monologue to Tim, telling him to stand perfectly still and not to move, not to try to turn round and go back inside – just to stay there and Mummy would be there in a second. Then there was the incredible moment of relief when we saw Mum's arms locked around him and we could breathe again.

And now here I was again. I looked at Mum and her eyes said to me, "Yes, I know what this reminds you of."

"If only someone could sneak up behind him," I whispered.

"It's impossible without going back to the car and driving round. But even that wouldn't do any good because the sound of a car would panic him."

"Do you think I should attempt to go down the middle of the two paths, Mum? That way I'd very soon be out of his sight. He wouldn't see me approaching."

"It's far too dangerous through there Lucy, and quite honestly even if you made it through to just below the bridge, how would you get up to him? I don't think you'd have the strength." I didn't press her any more. I have to admit, I was relieved she said no, because I'd never have dared anyway.

I don't know what made me turn round at that moment – just some inner feeling that someone was approaching. I thought my eyes were deceiving me, because who should be heading towards us but Andy and her dad. Where there had been one car, now there were two.

"How did you know where we were?" I asked Andy quickly because I was desperate to get back to Hal.

"I went round to your place and the twins

came rushing out from next door saying they'd got this brilliant idea that Hal would be here, because Miss Watkins had told them all about the superstitions surrounding this place and Hal kept on and on about it." Andy stopped talking abruptly and looked up at the bridge. Her big eyes stared in disbelief.

"Oh, my God," whispered Mr Sorrell, looking grimly up at Hal.

"We don't know what to do," I said to Andy. I lowered my voice. "We daren't go any nearer to him because he's threatening to jump."

"What about trying to get to him without him knowing?" Andy suggested. "You know, approaching him from the other side."

"There's no way except by car, and that would take too long," Mum answered.

"He'd realize what we were doing anyway," I pointed out, "if somebody went back to the car."

"Oh, dear, what are we going to do?" Mrs Perry asked. "I can't bear it a moment longer."

"What about down there? It's out of sight

of the bridge," Andy said.

"Nobody ever goes down there," Mum told her. "It's too dangerous."

"I'll go," Andy said, with that look on her face, the one I instantly recognized as the look which said, "Nothing will stop me now."

"You can't, Agnès," her father said, and for the first time I heard a note of fear in his voice.

"Just watch me," was Andy's deadly calm reply.

Nobody tried to stop her. There's something about that gritty courage in her, that defies challenge or opposition. She was wearing her black skirt and white shirt with a jacket on top. Not the best clothes in the world for dangerous rocky terrain. She zipped up her anorak and set off.

Hal might have noticed a tiny figure in the distance moving down from the upper trail to the lower track, but in no time at all, Andy would have been out of sight from the bridge, though we could all see her from where we were. Twice she slipped, the second time quite badly. There was an awful tense moment when she didn't get up straight away and I could see a muscle twitching in Mr Sorrell's face. The moment she got up and carried on, the muscle stopped twitching.

Like watching a tennis match, our eyes went from Andy to Hal, from Hal to Andy.

Miraculously, Hal hadn't appeared to move. Mrs Perry tried shouting again. "Please come down, love. We won't make you come back to us, but please get down from the side of the bridge."

"Where's my sister?" he screamed at the top of his voice, and the words seemed to echo round the valley and fill the air around us.

"We don't know, but we want to find her, too," I called back.

"You're just saying that," he yelled aggressively.

"No, it's true, I promise."

"Why hasn't anyone tried to find her before then?"

"Be careful," Mum warned me in an undertone. "Don't say anything to make him give up hope."

"Tell him the truth, dear," Mrs Perry said to me. "I can't shout any more. I just can't…" Her voice trailed away in despair.

"Let me come closer and I'll explain," I called.

"No, no closer," he said, injecting a new fierceness into his voice, and then horror of horrors he crouched down on the side of the bridge as though preparing to jump.

"OK. OK!" I screamed. "Your sister was taken to Canada with your parents…"

"They took her with them?" His words were so charged with shock and sadness that they only just reached me. He hadn't said, "And not me", but he might as well have done because the implication was so strong.

I clutched hold of Mum and said, "Oh no! I've said the wrong thing."

He was still in his crouched position and I wanted to say something, anything, that would give him a ray of hope.

"She may not be in Canada now," I called out carefully.

There was suddenly an extra layer of tension around me and I realized that Andy had reached the point where she was right underneath the bridge and she now had the most treacherous bit of her journey before her. She was climbing up on the other side of the bridge, so she could approach Hal from behind. I found myself crossing my fingers, then my arms and legs. Mr Sorrell seemed to be muttering something under his breath. Maybe he was praying. I'll never know. I've never mentioned that to anyone since.

"What do you mean?" Hal called out.

"We saw a girl on TV…"

"Is that true?" Mrs Perry asked, turning to me wide-eyed with disbelief. I nodded.

"We don't know if the girl we saw is anything to do with Hal," Mum began to explain.

"But it doesn't matter, if it's giving him hope," I finished for her.

"But he'll run away again, or do something even worse, if his hopes are dashed," Mrs Perry said, wringing her hands.

Again the awful feeling of despair came

over me as I looked into Hal's bleak future. It was true, even if we managed to save him from his grief today, there'd always be another day.

"What girl?" he asked, unable to disguise his interest, even with a fierce voice.

"It *might* have been your sister…"

"You're just saying that…"

"She was thirteen."

Hal straightened up. His action had the effect of making *us* all stand straighter as if now we were getting somewhere. But where was Andy? She should have appeared by now. Mr Sorrell's shoulders were hunched and his face looked grey and old.

"*So?*" Hal suddenly shouted with all his might.

"He's scared," Mrs Perry whispered, with a catch in her voice. "He's scared to believe you in case it all comes to nothing."

"I'm only telling you the facts," I called.

He was silent. My voice was aching from the strain of shouting. "Can someone else shout for a bit?" I asked Mum wearily.

"It's you he's pinning his hopes on. He won't listen to anyone else now," Mrs Perry added.

"You're doing brilliantly, Luce," Mum told me and I gave her a grateful smile. At the same time I wondered how much longer I could hold out saying the right thing. I have never felt so responsible for anyone in my whole life. I was wondering what to yell out next when we all gasped because the tiny figure of Andy had appeared on the bridge behind Hal.

"You're making it up!" Hal announced from his pinnacle and all our faces must have turned grey then because he dropped with great speed back into the crouching position as though to jump. It was more than Mrs Perry could cope with. With a stifled sob she hid her face in her hands.

"Call out something. Anything!" Mum instructed me, without taking her eyes off the scene ahead of us.

"The girl's name is Lucy," I screamed out at the top of my voice. "I promise. And Terry thought she looked like me…"

"Who's Terry?"

"My stepdad."

Andy seemed to be right behind him, but she had to climb up on to the side of the bridge and grab him, without letting him hear her.

"She'll never do it," Mrs Perry said. "She's too little."

"She's strong," I answered.

"And very determined," Mum added.

Mr Sorrell said nothing, just stood there, grey and tense.

What we witnessed next will stay with me for ever. Andy caught hold of Hal, and from where we were watching, they seemed like a pair of wrestlers, struggling and clinging to the bridge. Hal seemed to be pulling away from Andy and she was obviously trying to haul him back. As they lurched and rocked precariously, we stood and stared horrified and helpless, tears in our eyes, hearts in our mouths.

Then without warning they seemed to fall off the side of the bridge and on to the bridge itself and at that very moment a car pulled up beside them.

"It's going to hit them!" Mum screeched in horror, hiding her eyes in my shoulder.

"It's Terry," I breathed. "Look! That's Terry's car, I'm sure!"

Mum immediately jerked her head up to look. "Yes, yes it is!" she cried in wonder. And then we saw Terry get out of the car and bend down to Andy and Hal. There was a moment's stillness and then the sound of Hal's scream, only this time it was an unmistakable scream of joy.

"Whatever can Terry have said?" I asked Mum. She didn't answer. I think we were all too exhausted and dumbfounded to communicate any more. We waited till we saw the three figures on the bridge climbing into Terry's car, then without a word being spoken, the four of us turned and started the walk back to our own cars. My legs were like jelly. Mum and I linked arms and walked with Mrs Perry, but Mr Sorrell walked alone, eyes darting this way and that.

I realized after a moment that he was trying to pick up the sound of Terry's car. It wasn't long coming, and the sight of it pulling up beside the other two cars gave us all the boost we needed. With one accord our strange, breathless and bedraggled procession broke into a sort of half walk, half run.

Like a slow motion film Hal was heading towards us, dragging Terry along behind him by the hand. Poor Terry was trying, with obvious difficulty, to keep up. Andy had stayed by the car. As Hal drew closer to us, we could hear him shouting, but the rain was heavier now, and the wind was against us so it was impossible to tell what he was saying.

"Oh dear, he's all excited," Mrs Perry said as she ran towards her son. "I hope he's not pinning his hopes on the impossible."

"He actually seems happy," I said.

"Happy? He seems totally over the moon," Mum corrected me.

His high-pitched joyous scream became audible then. "Terry's found her! Terry's found her! Terry's found my sister! I've got a sister! I've got a real live sister!" On and on and on while poor, panting, unfit Terry struggled along in his wake. Hal's words seemed to spur us on because instinctively we all ran a bit faster.

"Oh, poor Terry," Mum began to laugh. "He never was the fittest man in the world!"

Her laughter broke down our fear and despair, and one by one we were all laughing, so that when Hal and his mother eventually collided with each other, and Terry went flying off at an angle, we were all reduced to mass hysterics. Our laughs and giggles and shouts of joy must have been heard from one end of the country to the other.

Mr Sorrell paused only to ruffle Hal's hair, then ran on to Andy. I watched as he swept her up in the air and spun her round, then brought her down and hugged her tight.

Hal was still jumping up and down around his mother, and chanting wildly, "Terry's found my sister. Terry's found my sister!" I went over to Andy and her dad.

"Thank goodness you're safe. It looked so

steep and slippery. You were brilliant, Andy," I told her warmly. "Even if you *were* totally crazy to attempt it!"

"No," Mr Sorrell disagreed. "*You're* the crazy one, Lucy. Andy is the *daring* one. And now I see why." Andy's bright eyes seemed brighter than ever because she'd done what she wanted to do – gained her dad's praise. He was looking at her so fondly that Andy looked like the happiest girl in the world. She also looked absolutely ridiculous with her torn tights, filthy, muddy clothes and sopping wet hair sending little streams of water down her face. Come to think of it, we must all have looked pretty ridiculous.

Terry and Mum were talking quietly at one side. I slipped up to them.

"Did you really find her?" I asked Terry, fearful of his answer.

"Yes, it's definitely her. One of the women in the office had taped the programme, so I got her to bring the tape in, then I watched that bit again, taking down the address and all the details. I phoned the BBC, because I knew

I wouldn't be able just to turn up un-announced at the home. The BBC then contacted the home, and the person in charge there phoned me to have a long chat. Afterwards I left the office for the rest of the day and drove as fast as I could to find the home. Three hours later I was face to face with Lucy and as soon as I began to talk to her, I knew the search had come to an end."

"So when can Hal see her?" I asked with impatient excitement.

"Tomorrow," replied Terry. "He and his mum and dad are going up there to meet her tomorrow."

Mum took Hal and Mrs Perry back home in her car, Andy went with her dad, and I went with Terry. We talked all the way. First about how Andy ought to be in the SAS, and then I made Terry tell me every detail about his meeting with Lucy. The bit where she hugged him and burst into tears of joy because she was finally going to really see her brother again, made me want to burst into tears of joy as well!

*   *   *

The next day at school was great because once we'd told Fen, Leah and Tash about the previous day's adventure, we all told our class tutors, and the teachers got together and decided to do a big extended assembly all about it. When we resumed normal lessons after break, our teachers said we were understandably too "high" to do proper work, so year eight had a great morning doing quizzes and things like that. I think it was actually the teachers who didn't feel like working. Mrs Merle was getting so carried away she was talking about contacting the national newspapers with the story.

I was asked over and over again to recount the story from my angle, but Andy finally had to have a quiet word with me when I started exaggerating and describing how she was hanging by only one hand from the bridge, and her free hand was clinging for dear life to Hal who was swinging below.

"Don't exaggerate, Luce, or no one will believe you when you tell the real truth," she sensibly advised me.

Fen sidled past and said out of the side of her mouth, "Nice to see we've got the old Luce back!"

At lunchtime we all sat together as usual with our packed lunches, and talked over and over the events of the previous day. Next we tried to imagine where Hal might be at this very moment. We wondered whether or not he would have actually met his sister yet.

"What if they don't like each other?" I asked, feeling really worried.

"They will. They're brother and sister," Leah said with quiet confidence.

"That's what I mean," I said half jokingly, thinking about Tim and Leo.

"Quite agree," Tash said, rolling her eyes and presumably thinking about her big brother Danny, who's fifteen.

"Me too," added Andy, who was obviously thinking about Sebastien, her two-year-old brother. Then she suddenly shocked us all by saying, "I'm really worried about Jan, you know."

Fen immediately sat up. "What do you mean, really worried?"

"I think the café might have to close."

"What?"

"Why?"

"How do you know?"

"Because I heard Jan talking to Kevin. I only caught the end of it... I can't even remember what she actually said now. I just remember thinking, 'Oh, no! No more jobs, no more Café Club...'"

"But why?" Fen demanded.

"Not enough customers. In fact yesterday there were hardly any customers at all. That's why I was allowed to go early."

We all gasped.

"But why?" Fen asked again, only this time she wasn't asking Andy, she was staring into the middle distance and thinking out loud. "Mum said we mustn't be too hard on Jan, didn't she, because she was going through a rough time? I wonder what she meant? I'm going to pump her for information tonight..." (Fen's mum is Jan's sister and they're very close. They talk about everything together.)

While the other five were pensively chewing their sandwiches I was yet again experiencing the collapse of my little world. I knew exactly why the café was losing business. It was because of me. The place had been full of regulars the day that Hal had loudly accused me of trying to abduct him from school. They obviously didn't believe Jan when she tried to smooth it all over afterwards.

"It's all my fault," I said, with another one of my famous sighs. The others looked at me sympathetically. I could practically hear their brains whirring, they were trying so hard to think of something to say to cheer me up. It was obvious why they couldn't think of anything – because they agreed with me. It *was* my fault.

"I'm sure you're not to blame," Tash finally said lamely, then went pink, which proved she didn't believe what she'd just said.

That evening I should have been so happy

and yet I felt such a failure. Mum and Terry could see I was gloomy, but I suppose they thought it was just the emotional anticlimax that had hit me. At five to seven the phone rang. It was for me. I took it upstairs.

"You won't believe what I've just heard," Fen began, breathlessly.

"What?"

"Tell you in twenty minutes. Can we have a meeting at your place? All of us?"

"Y–yes…" I said, hesitantly.

"Good, because I've told all the others. See you soon!"

Typical Fen. She makes decisions, carries out plans, then sorts out the rough edges afterwards. Something told me, from the sound of her voice, that though things were serious I wasn't directly involved. I ran down to Mum and Terry, clutching the phone with the aerial out, and said, "Is it OK if we all meet here in twenty minutes to put our project together?"

"I don't see why not…" Mum said, looking at Terry.

"Have we got a popular house or some-thing?" Terry said.

"The best!" I said, pretending to be in raptures.

"Go on then," he said, with a smile.

"Yes, that's fine," I said into the mouth-piece, then I paused for a count of three before saying, "OK, see you soon. Bye," and pushed the aerial back in. I knew they'd say yes, when it was obvious that I'd got one of my friends on the other end of the phone waiting. If they'd said no, I would have done a smart one by telling the imaginary person on the line that it didn't matter if we all got into trouble for not finishing our project, and that just for once I was sure it would be OK if we all got C plus... I know Mum and Terry. They would have cracked under that kind of pressure and let us do the project at our place.

By seven-thirty everyone had arrived, bearing files and books and looking very schooly. We spread it all out in front of us, for the benefit of any visitors to my room, then turned our full attention on Fen, who told us the following…

"Jan came round at six o'clock tonight, and it soon became clear that she and Mum didn't want me in the kitchen because Mum started dropping various unsubtle hints like, 'Haven't you got something to do upstairs, Fen?' So I decided to do a bit of earwigging outside the kitchen door.

"It wasn't easy because Emmy's latest craze is getting her big sister into trouble at every possible opportunity. It's to pay me back for taking three of her Rolos without asking her permission. So I knew I had to be very careful, because if she caught me outside the kitchen with my ear to the door, she wouldn't lose any time in telling Mum all about it.

"In the end – and you won't believe this – I pretended to be scrubbing away at a non-existent stain on the carpet right outside the door. Emmy watched me suspiciously for about five seconds, then said, 'Huh! Clumsy girl!' and flounced off, leaving me free to listen.

" 'All my regulars have deserted the place,' I heard Jan say.

" 'Because of Lucy?' Mum asked.

" 'No, because of me!' Jan answered. 'It was Kevin who told me,' she went on. 'He said he was working out at the gym, and there were two women in there. They'd no idea that Kevin was a chef or where he worked, and they were chatting away quite freely. One of them apparently said she wasn't going to go back to that café on principle. The other one huffily agreed and said it was perfectly clear that the manageress had got it in for that poor girl with the frizzy hair…' "

At this point I interrupted Fen's story of what she'd overheard because I wasn't too happy with that reference to my hair.

"Frizzy!" I protested loudly. "My hair is *not* frizzy!"

"No, I'm sure Kevin just forgot to mention that one of the ladies was as blind as a bat," Fen reassured me jokingly, before continuing her revelation.

"Anyway, Jan went on to say that these two

women in Kevin's gym talked for about five minutes about how they were going to stop going to the café because of the nasty manageress. They spoke quite scathingly about Hal too, apparently, but they forgave him, and said he was only a child and that they'd heard he had a lot of problems. They also made it quite clear that they were going to try to put other people off going to the café as well."

"Oh dear, poor Jan," Tash said, with typical generosity when Fen had finished.

Nobody liked to add, "And poor jobless us!" but I know we were all thinking it. At least that was what I was thinking at first, but very soon after, a brilliant plan started to take shape in my brain.

"I've got a great idea how to save the café!" I announced, and five pairs of eyes turned hopefully in my direction.

When the girls went home about half an hour later we were all feeling excited. I had been selected as the most appropriate one of us to approach Jan with our great scheme, and this I planned to do the following day after school. As it happened, though, I didn't have to wait that long, because the girls had scarcely been gone five minutes when the doorbell rang. I ran to answer it thinking someone must have left something behind, but there on the doorstep, stood Jan.

Chapter 10

"Hello, Jan," said Mum, who had appeared behind me. "What a lovely surprise," she went on in that sing-song voice that women often put on for other women. "Come in."

"I wondered if I could have a word with Lucy," Jan asked, her normal assertive tones sounding a little shaky.

"Yes, of course. There's no one in the den, Lucy."

The den is our cosy little box-room study which is my favourite room in our whole higgledy-piggledy house. I led the way. Jan was holding what I guessed to be Hal's letter. I was right.

"I owe you a big apology," she began. "I've been feeling guilty and terrible for quite some time." Then without further ado she handed me the letter. This is what I read.

Dear Manidjer Lady, I am the boy who came into your café with my mum and told a lie about that girl called Lucy. She never did try to take me away from school. I like her and thought she was my frend but now she is like the others and doesn't believe me so I am going away to a place that will bring my sister back to me, that will show everybody. I am telling you all this because that girl Lucy did not drop her tray she was carrying it very easily but I punched it very hard, very hard yes. She is nice and kind Lucy, she only told me a lie because she is sorry for me now I am sorry for her so I want you to tell her if was not her fault because the tray got punched very hard by me. From Hal.

Jan and I looked at each other for about five seconds when I'd finished reading the letter.

"I'm very sorry," she eventually said. "I've

got no excuse for assuming the worst of you every time anything happens."

"Yes, you have really," I tried to say, "because, let's face it, I *do* usually attract trouble, so no wonder you thought it was always my fault."

"And that's another incredible thing about you, Lucy – you're so forgiving. You forgave Hal despite all the aggro he caused you, and now you're forgiving me, and I've made your life so difficult lately."

"Fen's mum said we mustn't be too hard on you at the moment…" I began.

"Yes … that was something else, but that's all over now."

I didn't press her to say any more, so I stayed silent. "It was just that I thought I'd got myself a nice boyfriend," she explained all in a rush, "and I found that I hadn't, that's all… Well, he's a boyfriend, but he's not all that nice, and now he's not even a boyfriend so that's that." She shrugged wearily.

"Oh… I'm sorry…" I said, but I didn't want to talk any more about it, because it somehow seemed wrong to be discussing boyfriends with an adult.

"Anyway," she went on, "I wanted to apologize to you, but I also wanted to tell you that the outlook is grim at the moment. I was going to gather you all together but I decided that the least I could do for you after being so unfair was to tell you first.

"The thing is Lucy, it's because of the way I treated you, even though I tried to be discreet on each occasion. I obviously wasn't because customers are starting to feel that I'm being totally unfair to you, and they're stopping coming to the café. The regular hard core of customers has deserted me – and no wonder."

"Well, actually, *I* was going to talk to you about that," I began in my usual way, jumping in with both feet, "because the girls and I had this great idea of how to bring them back…" I trailed off because Jan was looking at me in a strange way. Then it dawned on me that she was trying to work out how the girls and I knew anything at all about this. Oh, dear. What could I say?

"Umm… Andy said there was hardly anyone there when she was working, you see… and…"

Still she was looking at me in that strange way, and I knew she hadn't bought my first attempt at an explanation, so I decided to go for a second attempt. This time the truth.

"Fen heard you and her mum talking," I confessed.

"I see," she answered, quietly. Then she smiled and the smile turned into a laugh. "That girl's ears must have some kind of radar device fitted to them," she joked, shaking her head in wonder. "OK, what's your plan?"

So I told her my plan.

"That's tomorrow!" she squealed.

"That's right."

"And when were you going to tell me?"

"First thing in the morning."

"Oh, the confidence of youth!" she said. "I suppose I should thank my lucky stars that I've got six of you to keep things in perspective for me," she said with a smile. "Right, let's get going, I think I'll start by phoning Kevin, then Debra, Becky and Mark."

"And I'll phone the girls."

"And we'll all meet at the café tomorrow at eight-thirty in the morning."

"Done!"

The next day, of course, was a Saturday. From the moment I opened my eyes I felt it to be a special sort of a day. There was something thrilling buzzing about in the air.

At eight-thirty we gathered together at the café and set to work. The rest of the girls and I compared posters. We'd done three each. Jaimini's were the best, because when God was giving out the brains, the good looks and the artistic streaks, the phone must have rung in the middle and he came back to work saying to himself, "Now where had I got up to? Had I already done this girl, Jaimini Riva? No, I don't think I had." But he had! So Jaimini got twice as much as her true share. That's my story anyway.

The six of us went round asking different

shopkeepers to display the posters in their windows for us, and a few of them were put in various other prominent places round the town. We'd also set a phone chain going from our parents through their friends, so that as many people as possible knew that this was the great day to come to the café.

Throughout the day the whole town would drop in and at some point the press would be there. We hoped that Hal would be there, too. There was no reply when we'd phoned the Perrys, but we'd dropped a letter in at the house, explaining what we were up to. Andy was the biggest attraction of all. It was our teachers who had given me the idea, because of the way they had reacted to our account of the events of Thursday afternoon.

We knew that Andy was a hero amongst her friends, of course, but we'd never realized just what an amazing thing she'd done. She had risked her life to save someone else's. Andy remained her usual quiet modest self, of course, only really caring that her dad was proud of her.

At ten o'clock we opened and by ten-thirty the place was bursting at the seams. Debra, Mark and Becky were going to be there as customers only. It was us six who were working all day. When Jan had bitten her lip and said, "I'm not sure I can afford all six of you," we'd assured her we didn't care about being paid.

"Look, Jan," Fen had pointed out, "the idea of this great promotion day is to get the café back on its feet. It doesn't even matter if we make a loss because of all the special offers, as long as we get business regenerated."

"Pardon me, Mr Murdoch," Kevin had said jokingly to Fen because she was sounding more and more like a business tycoon with every word, "but do I get paid for sweating my guts out in the kitchen, or what?"

"Yes, I think we can afford to pay the chef," Fen had joked back, adopting a posh, authoritative tone, which had given everyone a laugh.

By twelve-thirty it was clear that not only were we going to make a profit, we were going to make a big profit because people were leaving very generous tips which were mounting up in the jar behind the counter. "Looks like you won't have to forgo your wages, after all," Jan told us happily.

At one o'clock the local press arrived, which was part of our plan. Andy and I told the whole story. We made sure we were accurate in every detail, but we'd practised thoroughly, and were capable of giving a brilliantly breathtaking account even while sticking strictly to the facts.

"Where's the little boy?" the photographer wanted to know, but there was no sign of Hal. We even tried phoning his house but there was no reply. When the local press had gone there was a brief lull, then more photographers and reporters from other papers in the region turned up, as well as someone from local radio.

Andy and I were interviewed and photographed over and over again, and every time Andy generously said that she thought I'd played a much more important role than her

because in a way I'd been like a Fairy God-
mother to Hal. I thought that was a really
sweet way of putting it.

When all the media people had finally gone,
the café seemed less chaotic but it was still
chock-a-block with customers. Kevin came in
briefly to have a look round and to escape the
heat and steam of the kitchen. I noticed he
smiled and nodded at a couple of women
sitting at the little corner table.

"Have you seen who's over there?" he asked
Jan, in an undertone, as he went back into the
kitchen. Jan immediately went over to the
table that Kevin had indicated, and started
chatting happily. I realized it must have been
the two ladies from the gym. Good. If *they*
were back, all the regulars would be back,
because they were the kingpins.

After the hectic but wonderful lunchtime
period was over, later than usual, at about
four o'clock, we were a little less frantic. I
decided we ought to create a touch more
atmosphere so we started blowing up balloons
and trailing streamers and things.

Fen went out to buy some party poppers and she also bought a big party bag because I'd spotted little Ben Bridge with his parents and pointed him out to the rest of the girls, who all felt really sorry for him after his disastrous birthday party.

We filled the party bag with all sorts of sweets and goodies, and I personally presented it to Ben with great ceremony. His parents looked as though their beams had been painted on their faces since birth, and Ben's eyes widened in surprise and delight as he dipped in and pulled out this and that.

"May I have another Coke, please, Mum?" he asked as politely as ever.

"Sir can have anything he wishes," I grandly declared, then spun round with a flourish of my tea towel as though I were the King's chief butler or something, because by that time we were all totally high on the atmosphere. Unfortunately my arm knocked into the laden tray that Jan was carrying at the time, and everything came crashing down to the floor.

There was the briefest of stunned silences, then to the amazement of everyone in the café, especially the two regulars in the corner, Jan and I took one look at each other and exploded with laughter.

"Now the question is," Jan said in a loud comical voice, "did I drop that tray or was it knocked out of my hands?" Only the people who had actually witnessed the episode with Hal and my tray, understood her joke, but everybody erupted into laughter anyway, because they realized there was a good joke hidden somewhere in all the mess!

"Glad you haven't lost your touch," Mark commented, giving me a friendly nudge. With seven of us at it, it took no time at all to clear the mess and get back to normal.

I was standing with my back to the door wiping a table when I became aware of a change in the atmosphere. The chatter and laughter had softened to a buzz. I turned round and my heart stopped beating for a moment because there stood Hal. For such a wiry little kid he commanded one big bag of attention. The look in his eyes was positively triumphant. And no wonder.

At his side stood a girl of my height, with hair rather like a flatter version of mine. Her face had freckles like mine and her face was a bit thinner than mine, but she looked more like me in the flesh than she had done on television. She was dressed in really way-out clothes. She wore a long patched skirt with a thick tan belt at the waist and a faded orange shirt tucked into it. On top she wore a heavy brown waistcoat that looked about two sizes too big for her. Round her neck was a little scarf and on her wrist, loads of wooden bangles and friendship bracelets. Her foot-wear was a pair of very old DM's. I took all this in in a second. She looked mega.

Our eyes met and she gave me a faltering smile, then her features snapped back into neutral as though she was afraid to offer any more signals of friendship in case they were rejected. I scarcely had time to return her smile before Hal had run forward and hurled himself at me.

He put his thin arms round my waist, turned his head sideways and just stayed there in that fierce hug. I laid my head on his for a moment and it was as though his happiness was magically transferring itself to me. I'd never ever felt that feeling before. Then it was gone, and he was gone – back to his sister.

Hal took his sister's hand and dragged her over to me.

"This is Lucy," he said, "and this is Lucy," he added.

Lucy and I laughed and said "Hi". Then into the watchful silence erupted a great burst of applause which made me jump because for a moment I'd forgotten we were in the middle of a café!

"I want to…" Lucy began uncertainly, "…I mean, thank you for helping Hal find me…"

"No, it wasn't just me…"

"Yes, it was!" Hal insisted.

"No, because Andy…"

"But I can see why Hal thought you might be…"

"His sister?" I helped Lucy out.

"Yeah."

There was a brief silence because it's hard to know what to say first when you've got so very much to say.

"There'll be plenty of time for talking later," Mrs Perry interrupted gently, approaching our little circle exactly when we needed her.

"Just enjoy yourselves for a while," Jan said cheerfully. So we did. Old friends and new friends, slight acquaintances and complete strangers, all mingling happily.

When six o'clock eventually came, Jan put the CLOSED sign in place and Kevin emerged from his tropical quarters, wiping the sweat from his brow. Fen's mum and dad turned up, along with Andy's mum and dad, and my mum and Terry, and we all had our own private party.

Mr and Mrs Perry also appeared. It was the first time I'd ever met Mr Perry. He was very big and jovial. Mrs Perry seemed like a different person from the hunched and worried woman she had been two days before. She and her husband were cracking jokes and joining in loudly with all the songs that everybody was singing.

Hal's sister was quiet but she smiled a lot and wanted to hear the story of Hal and the Rolling Dippies from every possible angle. She studied Andy hard as we described how she'd managed the treacherous journey to the bridge. "But you're ... so..." she began.

"So little," we all chorused, nodding our heads and grinning.

"The thing is," Mr Sorrell said with a wink, "she's the daring one, so it doesn't matter how little she is."

"The daring one," repeated Lucy slowly, as though finding it difficult to cope with the culture shock of finding herself with these six weird girls.

"And it's true about Bengley Bridge. Miss Watkins was right!" Hal told us all. "It *does* make good luck come to you. I've proved it!"

We were desperate to hear Lucy's side of the story, but no one liked to ask in case it was hard for her to talk about her past. I decided to give her an opening.

"It was just so lucky that my family and I happened to be watching that documentary the other day, and saw you!" I said.

"I pinned all my hopes on that programme," Lucy told us in her quiet voice with a touch of a Canadian accent. You could have heard a fly sneeze when she said that, because she'd said so little up to that point and everyone felt curious about her.

"It's hard, you see…"

We waited.

"When you're only a kid…"

"Tell me about it!" I agreed wholeheartedly.

"You see, it took me all sorts of guts to leave Canada … and my parents… I mean after what they'd done…" (I liked the way she spoke. I liked the accent and the words she used, like "all sorts of guts".) "I couldn't live there, you see … knowing there was this kid brother – like – like left behind … you see."

We kept nodding. She was explaining something that was so far from anything that any of us had ever experienced that all we could do was nod.

"She was trying to find me all the time," Hal assured us.

"Too right, I was," his sister said warmly and the two of them moved a little closer to each other.

"Mum never really wanted to let you go, Hal," Lucy said softly to her brother. Hal frowned. "It was because of Dad, you see. Dad couldn't take to you. It happens sometimes … and after a bit Mum decided you'd be better off away from them where no harm could come to you. It broke her heart … but she did it for you…"

"And now you've gone, do you think her heart's broken in two places?" Hal asked innocently.

"I don't know," Lucy answered with a shrug. "All I know is that the break would be much bigger if she decided to leave Dad and come looking for us. It's weird with grown-ups, but for some reason, Mum just … loves Dad…"

236

Lucy stopped talking and suddenly looked tired out.

"Did you run away … back to England?" I asked.

"Yeah … I did."

Mum must have thought that Lucy had done enough explaining for now, because she suddenly said, "I propose a toast to Hal and Lucy – brother and sister!" And we all raised our glasses. The only trouble was that half of us hadn't got glasses, so some people had to raise anything that came to hand. Terry took a photo of us all and I knew it would be a competition winner when it was developed because Kevin had raised his tall chef's hat, Jaimini a note pad, Jan a plate with half a chocolate biscuit on it, and Mr Sorrell raised Andy herself and plonked her on the table in front of him!

"Do us a dance, Andy!" Kevin called out. "Go on, I *dare* you!" he goaded her.

She glared at him and said, "OK. I'll dance if you'll sing." So Kevin strummed an imaginary guitar, then clutched an imaginary microphone, and sang a ridiculous song with words that he was making up as he was going along, and by some miracle, every so often the words rhymed. Andy tapped and clicked and bounced and twirled while everybody clapped in time above their heads.

We gradually became aware that Jan was waving her arms about, not with reckless abandon, but to try and shush us. As the noise level went down, we could clearly hear that the phone was ringing so we stayed reasonably quiet for Jan to answer it.

Her side of the conversation sounded weird. She did a series of you-must-be-winding-me-up gulps, which reduced Becky and Debra to helpless giggles, then she exploded, "What! Now?" And after another couple of gulps she replaced the receiver.

We waited for her to tell us what was going on, and when she'd stood in a daze for about ten seconds, Fen's mum said, "Well?"

Jan shook her head as though to get herself out of a dream, then said, "Get ready to be famous everybody, we are about to have the company of several reporters and photo-graphers from various *national* newspapers!"

Her bombshell had the effect of putting the same dazed expression that Jan's face had worn a moment before on to all the faces in the room.

"You're famous, Hal," his mum said to him.

"You too, Lucy," added his dad.

"And Andy and Luce," added Hal.

"Don't forget Terry," said Lucy, whose favourite bit of the rescue story was the moment Terry appeared. She had a soft spot for Terry because it was he who had formed the very first link between her and Hal.

"I'd say we were a pretty famous bunch altogether," Terry laughed.

"What if…" Hal started to say, a look of panic flying across his face. Mrs Perry put one arm round Hal and one round Lucy.

"We'll sort something out," she said. "Don't you worry. But whatever happens, *nobody* is ever going to separate you two again."

Lucy still looked unsure of something.

"What is it, pet?" Jan asked, knitting her brow.

And at that very moment for some unknown reason I had a great idea about Jan. "I know," I called out enthusiastically. "Billabong!"

"What are you on about, Luce?" Jaimini asked me.

"Billabong!" I repeated. "For Jan! For a boyfriend!" I explained triumphantly because everybody was being peculiarly dim-witted all of a sudden. I grinned round but nobody seemed to have cottoned on to the brilliance of my idea so I went on a little bit. "He's Leah's tec teacher and he's absolutely gorgeous. In fact, I fancy him like mad, but I don't mind lending him out to you for a while, Jan…"

"Oh, shut up Luce!" about ten voices told me in unison, and no doubt I would have got even more stick if Lucy hadn't gravely asked, "I was just wondering, if Andy is the daring one, what's Luce?"

There was the briefest of pauses then, "One, two, three," said Kevin, and everyone

joined him in informing Lucy with un-
disguised glee and eyes rolling heavenwards,
"LUCE IS THE CRAZY ONE!"

Join

Would you and your friends like to know more about Fen, Tash, Leah, Andy, Jaimini and Luce?

We have produced a special bookmark to commemorate the launch of the Café Club series. To get yours free, together with a special newsletter about Fen and her friends, their creator, author Ann Bryant, and advance information about what's coming next in the series, write (enclosing a self-addressed label, please) to:

The Café Club
c/o the Publicity Department
Scholastic Children's Books
Commonwealth House
1–19 New Oxford Street
London WC1A 1NU

We look forward to hearing from you!

Anyway, back to the kitchen. I decided to elaborate on my day a bit, in order to find out whether Mum had any plans to send me to Finsbury Leighton, and also to give Cableden a big vote of confidence for her benefit.

"Actually, I had a brilliant day. Mr Waring is such a good maths teacher. In fact, it's only because of him that I like maths so much. Luckily, he'll still be my maths teacher next year, too."

I paused and glanced at her to see how she was taking it so far, but her hair was hanging over her face so I couldn't tell. I decided to carry on a bit with something that I just thought of that was completely made up.

"Oh, and great news! Leah is coming into my work group for maths and geography, and Tash is joining me for science. I'm really pleased because I know I see the girls at break, but it's not the same as being in the same work groups." Again I paused.

"Not Luce then?" she asked.

"No, we're only together for music, PE, drama and PSE."

"Well, never mind. When you're really good friends with someone, it doesn't matter if you're not always in the same class. In fact, it doesn't really matter if you're not even in the same school. After all, there are always the weekends and holidays."

I could feel my heart starting to beat faster. This sounded horribly like a lead into some dreadful announcement. I wasn't about to make it easy for Mum because there was no way I was going to any other school but Cableden, and she'd better know that.

"Weekends and holidays aren't enough, I'm afraid," I said firmly. "You see, your school is the most central part of your life. Well, for us six it is. That – and the café, of course."

"Hmm."

"What do you mean 'hmm'?" I suddenly

snapped at her. She didn't answer. "I *know* what you mean, anyway," I told her, raising my voice. That made her look at me properly. We faced each other across the kitchen with mounting anger hanging between us.

"Mr Waring let it slip about Finsbury Leighton, and I'll tell you right now, just in case you have any ideas about sending me there, I'm not going and that's that!"

"I'm not prepared to discuss it till your father gets home, then we'll talk about it sensibly, thank you very much."

"There's nothing to discuss. I'm not going."

Mum didn't answer so I went out of the back door, slamming it, then headed for Luce's higgledy-piggledy house.

On the way I could feel tears pricking at the back of my eyes, which really irritated me because my eyes are so big that the tears fall out more easily than they do with average-sized eyes. So by the time I was standing at Luce's back door I'd got three sodden tissues in my hand and there were two more big tears about to roll.

Goosebumps

by R.L. Stine

Reader beware, you're in for a scare!

These terrifying tales will send shivers up your spine . . .

Available now: